Take the Long

Way Home

Take the Long Way Home

Don Lombardi

"If you're the joke of the neighborhood, should you care if you're feeling good, take the long way home."

— Roger Hodgson

For Mama, who believed I could be a professional writer.

Acknowledgments

Elaine Lagarto - Editor

Elaine Lagarto - Cover Photo, Back Photo

Anna Mae Althen – Editor

Dr. Karen Jambeck, my favorite professor and source of inspiration

Dee Ann Donovan — Author's Photo

i

Table of Contents

Chapter 1: Can't Find My Way Home

Home—I've heard it said, "Home is a safe haven and a comfort zone, a place to live with our families and pets and enjoy with friends; a place where we can truly just be ourselves." The *Oxford English Dictionary* (OED) defines home as "a dwelling place; a person's house or abode, the fixed residence of a family or household, and the seat of domestic life and interests." The *Merriam-Webster Dictionary* pretty much echoes the same. "Home is where the heart is" likely is an old romantic adage. To me, home was just a place to lay my head. Home is not a magical feeling of belonging to something. It was a place not to be entered by those who didn't live there. Home was supposed to be a feeling that something belonged to me—I have never heard of a statement more untrue. Home was a place where we were supposed to feel safe. That certainly was not the case in my house.

My name is Ray MacDonald, and I was seven years old when I became aware of this place called home, and as far back as I can remember, it was not a nice place. It was fraught with anger and physical punishment—and poverty. Whenever my father decided the family needed a new place to live, we moved. This happened several times, beginning when I was seven until

I was around twelve years old. We must have moved to every low-rent street in Yonkers. I hated moving, and I hated my father. We moved so much that I grew to hate every new place we moved. It didn't matter where we moved; we could not allow ourselves to be comfortable, for if we did, it'd be time to move again. I remember moving to the Park Hill area; that was the Italian section of Yonkers. I thought we'd stay here for awhile, but no sooner did we get settled and we'd up and move again, this time to another "home", which was still in the Italian section. We moved yet again but stayed in the Italian section. The only good part was I got to stay in the same school. I never understood why we moved to the Italian residencies of Yonkers. According to my father, he knew some people in the area, but I never got to meet them. He claimed that one of his cousins lived there. Maybe this meant we would stay in one place for awhile, but I didn't bank on it. He could change his mind for no reason, and we'd have to move. There was no liking the placed we lived, as I thought we were on borrowed time.

I desperately wanted someone to be my friend, but neither I nor my brother were allowed to bring friends home, and because of that, I pretty much became a loner. There were kids at school who teased me about my clothes—they were second-hand, but my mother made sure they were clean and neatly pressed. Two boys I was somewhat friendly with told me to ignore those kids who made fun of me. I met Benny and Petey in second grade, and they proved to be decent guys, but I was accustomed to waiting for the ball to drop and have them turn on me. I didn't enjoy school; I just attended. The only subject I liked was writing—at least, I could write my thoughts and feelings. I recall writing stories and poems about places I'd never been, wishing that my stories would take me away, at least for a little while. I daydreamed about a place where I could write poems and listen to music all day. I dreamed about being a musician when I grew up and having a guitar. They were only dreams and daydreams of a lonely, scared boy, but to me, they were dreams about my future. I wouldn't be a small boy forever. I would grow up someday into manhood, and no one would hit me then. Until that time came, I was under my father's rule.

I remember one place we lived where my father had this sick crush on a lady named Ruthie, who lived upstairs with her six children. I didn't see the attraction, but anything she wanted done, my father would jump to it. I noticed one day, in particular, she was talking to her sister about my father and laughing about him being her personal lap dog. My father told me once privately that Ruthie and he had kissed. I didn't need to hear that. Why was he kissing some other woman when he was married to my mother? Whatever the reason, it only made me hate him all the more. We moved again shortly thereafter,

3

although this time, I was glad that we moved far away from Ruthie. Her kids weren't friendly with my brother and I and suited me just fine—I didn't like them anyway.

It took me awhile to figure it out, but it appeared that my father had trouble holding a job and paying the rent. Every time he was out of work, my father delivered punishment to me and my brother more frequently. I wondered so many times why my father hit me and my brother so much. What made him this way? Why would anyone hit someone they supposedly loved? I was a sensitive boy, and I cried easily—my brother was tougher than I, but I remember seeing him cry after my father punished him. I recall planning to run away to my Aunt and Uncle's house where you could count on one hand how many times my uncle or aunt got angry. These were good people. Sometimes I would wish that I could live with them, but then my mother would be left to my father's abuse. I never followed through with that plan because I had no money to get on the bus. I could have earned the money to run away, but the real reason I chose to stay was for my mother. She wasn't a strong woman, but she loved me and my brother.

No matter where we moved, home was a place where my father liked to dish out what he called 'discipline', but it was really "punishment." He didn't know the meaning of either word, and he really didn't care who got hit once he started swinging his belt. His belief was simple but most unfair: You punish one, then you punish two. So, it didn't matter who did something wrong. The other child who did nothing wrong was punished regardless. At times, my mother shielded me from being hit by my father, thereby taking the hit for me. This was a common occurrence. I think my father's anger started in childhood and was further developed in the Marine Corps during the Second World War, but I still don't know why he took his anger out on his family. He had no problem making my mother his punching bag. All I remember was my mother and I being hit for no reason—I was too scared of my father to do anything wrong.

If I wasn't being "disciplined" by my father's hand, I was writing little stories and poems for school or listening to my father play the radio or his records. As long as I remained quiet, I figured I wouldn't get hit for nothing. My father had his favorite songs and artists—not always my favorites, but I listened to every word of every song until I became a walking jukebox. My father liked to put me on display to family and friends. Come see the walking jukebox who knows all the words to every song he's heard. I really didn't care for being on display, but at least I wasn't being hit—at least for now. My brother had a transistor radio from which I learned most of the songs like "Duke of Earl" by Gene Chandler. I wasn't about to give my father credit for teaching me the songs I heard—

music meant too much to me. I pretended to be in a row boat when I heard "Michael, Row the Boat Ashore" by The Highwayman or in a motor boat when I heard "26 Miles" by the Four Preps.

I loved music, especially Rock & Roll, and being that my father was always playing the radio or the record player, I listened intently to each song. I liked mostly every piece of music I heard, from Rock & Roll to Classical to Blues. My mind was like a sponge when it came to music. I did well in school and obeyed my father's every command, but I was confused. We listened to music together, yet he'd change in an instant when he decided to give me a shellacking for no apparent reason. I did everything I could to stay out of my father's way, which he used as an excuse to hit me or my brother. Maybe he didn't want me to get to know him when he saw how much I loved music, that it might bring me closer to him, but that was a foolish thought. There was no getting close to him, and so I just stayed out of his way.

I remember the talent show that took place at school. We had to get permission from our parents to sign up. My brother Joe and I got permission slips and ran home to get our parents' blessing. My father stood firm with a no—we were not permitted to do what he called "stupid things" like a talent show. My mother disagreed and told him that she would give her permission for us to compete in the talent show. My father just waved his hand as if to say he didn't care. I was not surprised by his attitude, but my mother's defiance surprised the hell out of me.

Joe and I sang with three other boys as a group. We did well, but we didn't win anything. It wasn't important that we win, I just wanted to make my mother proud. After the show, I met a boy named Danny—he played the electric guitar in the show, and that fascinated me. He invited me to his house a few days later and taught me three guitar chords—not bad for a fourth-grader. I didn't have a guitar, but I was psyched about learning my first chords. After that, I could think of nothing else but playing the guitar.

I continued to visit Danny at his house until my father put the kibosh on it—I couldn't even visit my new friend. I had to tell Danny that my father wouldn't let me come over to his house anymore. When Danny asked me "why", I could only say, "That's the way my father is", and I dared not go against him. Danny and I were both disappointed; I think he liked teaching me the guitar and having my friendship.

My father continued to ruin any type of activity I wanted to be part of—it was like if he wasn't part of it, Joe and I couldn't be part of it. This really frustrated me since whatever I chose wasn't hurting anyone. At any rate, I kept my distance.

Chapter 2: Rock & Roll High School

I was twelve years old when The Beatles burst onto the music scene, and I was totally blown away by their music, their clothing, and their accents. I saved all the money I could from running errands for neighbors and from relatives and for my First Holy Communion and Confirmation in a small savings account. I had enough to buy an inexpensive acoustic guitar from Bill's Music shop and a pair of "Beatle boots" from Flagg Brothers Shoe Store. My father didn't seem to care what I got so long as he didn't have to pay for anything.

After I did my homework each day, I spent the rest of my time trying to teach myself the guitar. Those were the times I loved trying to write a song or trying to learn a piece from the radio. That guitar became everything to me. I didn't really learn much from fiddling around with the guitar. I just enjoyed trying to play it. The day came when my father had enough of me and my guitar, and he smashed it to pieces. I was heartbroken, and I cried like a baby. In a fit of anger, I yelled at him, "Why did you do that? My guitar wasn't hurting you." He raised his hand as if to slap me, and I said, "Go ahead; you can't hurt me anymore." He said, "Yeah? Well, you don't bring anything in this house unless I say so, understand?"

To say the least, music bought me a short-lived amount of pride from my dad. My brother called me a brown noser, though I tried to tell him I was just staying out of my dad's way. With every snap of my dad's belt, I prayed for it to end. After a while, I began liking my beatings to a crucifixion. The beatings were severe and didn't stop with the belt. My dad took particular pleasure in beating my small hands with his big, powerful, and rugged hands. This did not help my ability to write or play the guitar. Mom loved to see what I wrote for school or pleasure. My dad thought of me as a sissy. There was no pleasing him, and praying did nothing to help the situation. It was then that I decided there was no sense believing in a God who allows children to be hurt, and every beating only solidified my belief.

My mother first taught me about God when I was about four or five years old, and I hung on to every word she said. God sounded so wonderful, and at that age, I soaked up everything my mother taught me like a sponge. But where was God when I was beaten at my father's hand? I didn't understand. If I hadn't done anything wrong, why did I have to take a beating, and why did God allow this to happen? Eventually, as I got older, the questions stopped, as there were no answers to be had. Fortunately, as I aged, the beatings also stopped, but that didn't mean I started believing in God. It simply meant that I grew bigger than my father, whose small frame stood at five feet and three inches. My mother tried to convince me that being beaten was not God's fault. Maybe not, but where was He when I needed Him? I really wanted a close friend, but I was the brunt of the jokes from most kids my age.

I learned a few guitar chords from a school chum, and he gave me a printed sheet of guitar chords so I could learn and practice on my own. Speaking of friends—My father's law was to never bring friends into our house, so my whole school experience was not to include friends. I saw my schoolmates hanging out with their friends and having fun, and I wanted the same, but it wasn't in the cards for me so long as I lived under my father's roof.

Oddly enough, my brother did as he pleased, sometimes without punishment. My guess was as long as it pleased my father, it was allowed. After all, he was the firstborn son. The only thing my brother and I had in common was music. He was as much a Beatles fan as I am. That being said, he shielded me and my music activities from my dad. If I were to get a paying gig at the library or some other daytime gig, he would say that I was in music class at school if my father asked. It cost me a few bucks, but it was worth every penny. I made a few dollars and socked away every cent of it for an electric guitar. I figured it wasn't bad for a kid about to turn thirteen—and I didn't have to give it to my father or God.

I met another guy through my brother who played the guitar. He went to a different high school, but we became fast friends and shared guitar knowledge with each other. Tom taught me Beatle songs that I wanted to learn, and in return, I taught him Barre Chords, which every guitar player has to know. After learning about thirty songs, Tom and I talked about starting a band. We thought we'd make a few bucks and meet some girls. Both were equally important. Tom already owned an electric guitar, but I needed to get one soon. I had about fifty dollars saved, and Tom thought I could get an electric guitar at Woolworth's. Those guitars are made in Japan and aren't very good, but they get the job done. Next, we had to get amplifiers for the guitars. I borrowed one from a friend, and for a while, we both plugged into the same amplifier—not the best hookup, but it would have to do. Tom got an amplifier soon after, and things started to look up. He managed to get us a drummer. Dennis was a real powerhouse with a set of champagne Ludwig drums. We started having rehearsals at a Baptist church hall, and we even managed to get a few gigs at that church. We didn't make more than a few dollars each, but we were playing gigs and getting paid. The first few gigs we played didn't make us enough for car fare, so we donated it to the church. So much for God not getting the money.

High school was, in a word, painful. Aside from not wanting to be there, I had to put up with a barrage of comments from my schoolmates. One of them yelled out in a hall full of my classmates, "McDonald's a pauper." By my clothing alone, anyone could tell that I came from a low-income family, but somebody advertising my poverty wasn't necessary. I wanted to be accepted by my schoolmates, but after hearing someone's discontent with my economic position, the best I could do was to stay under the radar until I was old enough to leave school. Yes, even in the eighth grade, I knew that I would be leaving school early. One of my classmates mentioned that there was going to be a Sadie Hawkins dance next Saturday where the girls selected the guys rather than vice-versa.

I had no intention of going just to be embarrassed by some mean adolescent, but somehow I was talked into going to the dance. I looked through my closet at home to see what I could wear to the dance without causing myself any type of humiliation. By the time Saturday rolled around, I was a bundle of nerves, and I went back and forth about going to the dance.

I finally decided to go to the dance—if for nothing else than to pick up some of the songs that the band played. The band was called The Trend, and from the first few songs they played, this band was good. I was okay being a wallflower and just listening to the band. All of a sudden, a girl was coming toward me. I didn't recognize her.

Then she introduced herself as Sally and asked if I'd like to dance. What a joke. I didn't know how to dance, and I told her so. She said, "That's okay. Just go with the beat." I understood that, but Heaven help me; I let Sally lead me to the dance floor. Fortunately, it was a slow song, and I just felt the beat and went along with it. Sally and I sat and talked for a while until she heard a song that made her want to dance. After a few songs, we went outside to get some air. She was easy to talk to. After talking about our habits and hobbies, it turns out that she knew my aunt, Edie, from church—talk about a small world.

As the dance came to an end, Sally and I exchanged phone numbers, and then I asked how she was getting home. She said that she only lived a few blocks away, so she was walking. I asked if I could walk her home, and she said yes. We talked as we walked to her house and, as we arrived, I asked if I could see her again. Once again, she said yes. Then out of nowhere, she kissed me—on the lips. Yow, my first kiss! We said good night and that we'd talk soon. As I walked home, I couldn't get Sally out of my head. She was so beautiful, and my hand-me-downs didn't seem to matter to her. I met this lovely girl at a Sadie Hawkins dance, and I wasn't even trying. Sally and I dated casually through high school. Sometimes we saw a movie and went for pizza afterward.

We went to a lake once with her folks. They were so nice to me. Every date with Sally was as great as the first time we met. I don't think I'd ever met a kinder person. Then she graduated and went off to college, as she was two years older than me. Somehow we lost touch for a while, and I didn't hear from her for almost two years. College must be demanding. She told me that she met a guy in college, and they were going steady. I wasn't crushed, but I'd hoped we'd see each other more after she graduated from college, but that didn't appear likely. Thanks again, God. As if my life wasn't screwed up enough already.

As I mentioned earlier, high school was a painful experience, and I couldn't wait to get out of it. I was sick and tired of being the brunt of my schoolmates' jokes and all the teasing about my secondhand clothing. My mother did the best she could with the little money she had to buy me school clothes. Some of them came from relatives, and some came from thrift shops and the Salvation Army, but my clothes were always clean and neatly pressed.

Chapter 3: Army Times

Having had enough of school and everything about it, I dropped out at age sixteen. This saddened my mother, but my father couldn't care less. I took a full-time job at Kleinmart department store, and they assigned me to the record department. I was pleased with my assignment. I only made about sixty dollars a week, but it was enough to save for my electric guitar and amplifier and to give my mother a few dollars, which benefited the household. Along with that, I paid for my own clothes and daily meals. It eased my mother's mind knowing that I could take care of myself. I'd left school, but I had every intention of getting an equivalency diploma. I didn't know how or when, but it would really make my mother happy to know that education was important to me. I managed to get a job at Kleinmart department store. I worked there until I turned seventeen. It was sure fun working in the record department. I made a few friends while working there who included me in their after-work activities.

Tom joined the Army and was about to ship out. His reason for joining the Army was to get an education. I joined about a month later for the same reason. As part of our enlistment contracts, Tom would be going to Texas for Medical Corpsman training, and I'd be headed to Georgia for

Radioman School. I wasn't pro-military or anything, but I could get a high school diploma while still in basic training. I said my goodbyes to my family and promised my mother that I'd write frequently. Next stop—Fort Jackson, South Carolina. For the most part, basic training was like being at home; only it was a drill sergeant yelling at me instead of my father. Not much I could do about that, but it'd all be over in eight weeks, and then I'd be off to Radioman advanced individual training.

In the meantime, basic training was more hurry up and wait than anyone could stand. Drill sergeants constantly yell at you as you drop everything you're carrying and fall on your face for every three steps you take. At any rate, I just kept thinking, "Just a few more weeks."

One night during basic training, Drill Sergeant Washington comes down the company street, "four sheets to the wind," stopping in front of my barracks at 0300 hours and calling my name, "MacDonald—Private MacDonald, bring your young ass out here right now,

"Yes, Drill Sergeant, Private MacDonald reports as directed."

He says, "Lombardi, I like you," as he puts his arm around me.

"Oh my God", I said to myself—I hope he doesn't like me that much.

He says, "Lombardi, I hear you were a singer in civilian life."

Oh no, I said to myself, "Lombardi, he said, "I want you to sing me a Beatle song." You like the Beatles, right?"

"Yes, Drill Sergeant, I like the Beatles."

He says, "Lombardi, I want you to sing "I want to hold your hand"."

So there I was, singing "I want to hold your hand" to a six feet four inches black Drill Sergeant at three o'clock in the morning. Meanwhile, all the other guys were hanging out the windows laughing their asses off. The next day and for the rest of basic training, I had to put up with names like 'Caruso' from trainees and Drill Sergeants alike. This might have been the toughest part of my basic training. The rest of basic training seemed to have flown by as we got together on the last night for a beer party hosted by none other than Drill Sergeant Washington, who insisted that I sing a song for the guys. With no way out, I finally relented. The next day, we graduated basic training.

Next stop, Fort Gordon, Georgia. From the 'get-go', ten weeks of Radioman school was enough to knock the wind out of my sails. It was just like basic training, only a lot more technical. The Non-Commissioned Officers still yelled at me during regular intervals, and then there was field training. It was complete with my field gear, M16A1 Rifle, and a twenty-five-pound PRC-25 Radio. I collapsed on my bunk after three days of field training, only reviving myself for food and a shower.

After the training portion of my military service, I got thirty days' leave before reporting to Oakland, California, for overseas duty in the Republic of Vietnam. Part of it scared the hell out of me, and it terrified my mother. My father could care less. While I was on leave, I did my best to do absolutely nothing. This got my father steamed—he thought I should be working and giving him half my pay. I made it very clear that I now worked for the U.S. Army, and I owed him nothing.

I met a girl while on leave, and we hit it off right away. Her name was Susan, and she was beautiful. She promised to write every week and that she'd be waiting for me when I got home—hmm, we'll see. I was off to the Republic of Vietnam at the end of the month. A tearful goodbye with my mother, a handshake from my brother, and not a single word from my father. Maybe it was better that way. Okay, God. This is your last chance. Let's get me home alive, Okay?

Chapter 4: In Country

We're here—Vietnam at the 90th Replacement Battalion on an airbase called Bien Hoa. It's one of two places where incoming troops land when they get in a country before being sent to their assignments. The other is Cam Ranh Bay. The smell of aviation fuel and the faint odor of a Vietnamese woman cooking something that smells like dead fish left out in the sun are just samples of what is filling my lungs. There is a stench that I can't describe that's making me nauseous. God, I think I'm about to vomit. The stench I can't describe is actually just a few feet away. It's the smell of dead soldiers inside body bags out in the hundred-and-ten-degree sun, waiting to be loaded onto a stateside-bound aircraft.

Aside from the stench of the fermenting bodies, getting off the plane in Vietnam was an immediate education in tropical climates. I don't mind the warm weather, but the heat here is so intense you can actually see the heat waves rising off the runway. It's like walking out of an air-conditioned room into a blast furnace. Right off the plane, somebody was always yelling at me to do something—either to clean this or pick up that. I feel more like a janitor than a soldier.

Man, is it hot or what? So, this is where all the newbies go when they get here. This freaking guy tells me to do this and that and starts yelling, "What are ya? Stupid?" I wanted to punch his lights out, but he had more stripes than me, and so here I am, cleaning up in this colossal freaking heat wave. Some soldier I am—PFC Raymond J. MacDonald, a freaking janitor. I swear, if I had to defend myself, I'd have to use a broom or a mop. Now that would be a real contribution to the war effort.

God, they must do this to everybody who comes to Nam. Bust the newbies' asses for 25/8 and generally give us a hard time and a bad day for about three months or until we spill some blood. They had me burning shit in fifty-five-gallon drums that were cut in half. I had to mix kerosene with the piles of human excrement so it would burn well. Then I filled sandbags from noon till chow and policed up the area of operation until I was eating dirt. It's an initiation, I guess, to see if we're worth it. If you buy the farm within the first three months, then obviously, you're as worthless as tits on a bull. They'll remember you, but only for a little while. If you manage to stay alive amid the disease and the bullets, then you're okay, and you have the right to carve a handhold among them until you rotate back to the world—either with orders or a toe tag.

Did I mention disease and bullets? Well, we also got bugs, meaning that we have flying cockroaches that attack you in squadron formation. I hear some guys even shoot the little bastards. And then there are tigers in the jungle, along with the two-step snakes that camouflage so well that they look like bamboo. They call it a two-step because if it bites you, then two steps later, you're dead—no antidote, just plain dead. Amen, I swear.

The only way to get around Vietnam is to hitch a ride on a chopper or take the shoe leather express. I've only been in the country for forty-five days, and walking around this place gives me no level of comfort, so I opted for the helicopter route. I'm still going through strange places, but faster and without sore feet. I managed to hitch a ride on a Huey headed to Saigon. Good thing because that's where I need to go.

It's a real heartache trying to get supplies out in the field. They're either three days late or not what we needed. Desperate measures being what they are, we have to employ other tactics, like bartering or liberating supplies from a field hospital that has "too much" of this and "not enough" of that. I don't know why they picked on me to get the supplies. Guess they figured I'd have to do it sooner or later. All I heard was, "You, newbie!" and a half dozen heads turned.

"Not you!

"Hey, you, New York. What's your name?"

"MacDonald. Who's asking?"

"Me, your squad leader. Time for you to go to Third Field Hospital and pick up supplies. The chopper is late, and we can't wait until the slick decides to show up, so grab your gear and flag down a chopper on the crap table. Pick up some supplies and head over to Firebase Doomsday."

I was on the helipad, known as the crap table, in a heartbeat. I was going to Saigon for supplies. Oh yeah, I'm going to Saigon to get supplies—right after, I'll stop at the massage parlor.

We were flying along without incident when the pilot took the chopper up to about six thousand feet. It was so peaceful that you'd never think we were at war. It was cold too. The clouds at that high an altitude looked like mashed potatoes in the sky until you flew through one of them, at which time you realized there was a wad of condensation that threw the rotor blades out of wack and made for a very bumpy ride. As we continued, one of the crew motioned to me to hang on. I nodded and just let my baby blues peruse the wild blue yonder.

All of a sudden, we began to lose altitude. The ship was literally falling out of the sky at a slow rate of descent like the chopper was a sheet of paper that someone dropped. I was terrified. I thought, "Holy shit! We're going to crash! Is this what it feels like before you die?" It felt so freaking weird. It's like you have time to recollect but no time to do anything about it. Then, in what seemed to be the blink of an eye, the chopper began to fly steady and level. I didn't know what to think.

Later, after listening to the crew laughing their asses off, I learned that what happened was called Autorotation. It was done on purpose to "break my cherry," so to speak. Eventually, we were flying over the South China Sea at around five hundred feet, something they call flying "feet wet." It was really cool. The rotor blades turned at thousands of revolutions per minute. The patterns of the sea below me changed each time the ship changed direction, and it pissed off the sharks too.

Sometimes the gunners went hot on the sharks. Some of them have been known to leap out of the water, but mostly the gunners went hot on the sharks simply to vent. They just needed something to kill. As we started to move inland just outside Saigon, we took small arms fire from the ground. The gunners opened up right away with return fire. It seemed never to end. I kept seeing muzzle flashes on the ground and shell casings next to me. One of the gunners got hit in the leg—a small piece of shrapnel or a bullet from the size of the wound—but he was bleeding pretty badly. I tried to treat his injury while we were still under fire, but I only managed to apply a field dressing to the wound. I was amazed that he didn't stop firing the machine gun even though he was wounded. He just kept saying "aw shit" and "fuck it" a lot, shrugging it off until the firing stopped. God, all I wanted was to get to Third Field Hospital.

I was not ready for this, but something one of my uncles used to say came to mind: "When you're up to your butt in alligators, that's when you remember your objective was simply to drain the swamp." Except that half the damn country was a swamp. "Fuck it. Don't mean nothing." They say that a lot here, but I don't know why just now. Oh my God, what's happening? My leg hurts. It's burning—Holy shit, I'm hit! Look at that blood. I never bled like this before, and it's not like a shaving cut. I always wondered what it would be like. Now I know for damn sure. So many thoughts are racing through my head: "Am I gonna die? Will I bleed to death? What if the chopper gets hit? Will they take me prisoner or just kill me? God, please don't let me die in this place. Mama, I'm bleeding, and it hurts so bad. Please, Mama, make it stop! Please make it stop!"

The flight to Third Field Hospital seemed longer than usual. It felt like an eternity, even though I'd made the trip a hundred times. I was half-conscious and not able to make out what the crew was saying, but it sounded like they were talking about me. There was blood all over the ship, mine, and everyone else's. I'd lost a lot of it, which was probably the reason I was half out of it. Still, I wished I knew what they were saying. I'd heard blood was like motor oil for the body. Well, it must be true, because it had a stench, or maybe blood just smelled like that when you got wounded. Either way, it didn't smell pretty. I thought a lot about dying. Did that bullet have my name on it? Was it my time to go? No way! It was only a leg wound. I wasn't going to die in Vietnam. It was such a beautiful country but so full of evil. Had that made me evil? I had no answer, and I was so tired. I saw too many men die in combat or strung out on drugs or alcohol. We were all afraid, and we just wanted to get out of Nam.

We made it to Third Field Hospital. Big freaking hero I am. I passed out in the chopper. It seems I lost a good amount of blood. We're alive, and the gunner is okay. He thanked me for patching him up under fire. He said it took guts to do that—told his AC to put me in for a medal. Mama would be proud, but to hell with the medal—I'm just glad to have my gonads intact. God, I just wanna pick up supplies and get back to Firebase Doomsday in a big-time hurry, but it doesn't look like that's going to happen today. They pulled a piece of shrapnel out of my leg and patched me up nice and clean. It hurt like a mother. They're keeping me here at Third Field overnight just to make sure the wound doesn't get infected. It feels good to sleep in a real bed, and some of the nurses looked oaky, but unless you're an officer, you ain't gettin' a piece of nothin' except air, so it's goodnight from beautiful downtown Third

Field Hospital. What the hell did I get myself into? I get hit the first day in the country, and there goes my massage. Nice going, newbie. You really made yourself a shit sandwich this time.

I can't believe this, but I should. I got a paper bullet. That's what we call a "Dear John" letter in Nam from a wife or girlfriend who didn't have the common decency to wait for the guy to come back before telling him that it was over between them. Too many guys got these letters and ended up eating a bullet over some girl who wasn't worth it. I've been in the country less than a week, and now I got this paper bullet from Susan, who I dated briefly while on leave prior to coming to Vietnam. She said her reason was that she couldn't be involved with someone who could get killed. Gee, so who gets the raw end of this deal? Is she afraid? She has no idea about being scared. I wasn't going to justify her letter with an answer. The best thing I could do for myself is to put Susan out of my mind as if she never existed. Fuck it. Don't mean anything.

Chapter 5: Common as the Rain

Vietnam was a strange country and a paradox—a rose with many thorns. Romantic places like Vung Tau or the Caravelle Hotel conjured up images of grandeur from the French colonial period. The majesty of the mountainous central highlands, similar to the Appalachians, was home to deer and Montagnards, but then there were the scars from B-52 strikes and artillery fire in a war that couldn't be won without the support of the people, and they didn't want us there. Why should they? We impregnated their women, stole their drugs, and killed their people. Their economy thrived on what we soldiers spent on women, drugs, and alcohol and from what we sold on the black market. Some called this fighting Communism.

Holy shit, I woke up in hell, and it was white with ugly nurses. A million thoughts went flying through my head. I had a leg wound that didn't look good. I remembered reading about soldiers during the Civil War who had to have their legs cut off after being shot. God, I couldn't lose my leg. I saw soldiers every day who'd stepped on land mines or gotten hit by a 51-caliber round. I felt for them. It was strange, but I thought about Gator and Blackjack. They both got hit badly and died while I was trying to patch them up, waiting for the Medevac to come.

I did what I could, but there wasn't much left of either of them. Half of Blackjack was splattered forty feet away from the rest of him after he'd stepped on a Bouncing Betty and Gator—well, he got ripped in half by a burst of 51-caliber fire. We couldn't even find his legs. It might sound terrible, but I believe it was better that they died quickly. Every wound was serious, but when I first got there and saw soldiers who'd lost an arm or leg, I thought, "My God, they have to go through the rest of their lives like that. Was there a girl somewhere who would still want somebody with an arm or a leg missing? What would their parents think? How would they feel when people looked at them? How would they feel when they were alone?"

Lying in that hospital bed felt like living in perpetuity. Doctors and nurses passed by all the time. Most of them didn't even look at me. It was as if I didn't exist. Maybe they didn't want to feel anything—no pity, no anger; just do the job. Don't become too attached to the soldiers because they were in and out of the hospital pretty quickly. If the staff allowed themselves to feel something, it would tear them up if a soldier died, and if the soldier went home, he would be missed. And no one wanted the patient to return to the place where death occurs in the blink of an eye.

After what must have been days, somebody who resembled a nurse finally came to check on me and the bandages on my leg. She was definitely female, and she smelled good. The rest of the place had the typical hospital antiseptic smell mixed with blood, shit, and dead flesh.

"How do you feel?"

"With my hands, howdya' think?"

"It sounds like you feel better—you make fun of me."

"I'm not making fun of you. I'm just trying to stay alive. I wasn't trying to hurt your feelings."

"Is okay, GI. I know you scare after get hurt, but you be okay, then maybe you go home. No more fight, no bombs, nobody kill, no more Vietnam."

"Yeah, ya gotta keep movin' ahead. That's what I always say."

"Where your home is? I can't say your name."

"Ray MacDonald, but call me Mac. I'm from New York, the Bronx. Yonkers, to be exact."

"Yonkers? How can City be Island?"

"Hey, it's New York. Anything can be anything."

"What kind of name is, Mac, MacDon—?"

"MacDonald. It's a Scottish name. And what do they call you?"

"Lanh. My name Lanh."

"What's the rest of your name?"

"Lanh Huy Tien," she mouthed softly from her full lips. "Have to go. I see you later, Mac."

"OK, Lanh."

Lanh Huy Tien—guess they didn't send all the ugly nurses here after all.

What was it that she said? "—maybe you go home, no more fight, no bombs, nobody kill, no more Vietnam." Hmm! Lanh was bright, but she didn't have a clue as to what going home would be like. I had no regrets about leaving Yonkers, but I missed my mom. She'd be all right as long as she still got my allotment checks. My lazy bastard father hadn't worked in years. He'd been taking the money that I sent to my mom right up until I graduated from paratrooper school. I set him straight after that. He would never hit her again or take the money I sent her. The bastard was as useless as tits on a bull. Ever since he got out of the military, he just sat on his butt all day, watched television, and smoked cigarettes. Maybe he'd choke to death on them someday.

Lanh smiled a lot, but I sensed a distant unhappiness about her. She gave the kind of half smile that hid pain or sadness. There was no talk about her past, and she tended to change the subject when I asked about it. Her parents were both dead, but

I didn't know if it was war-related or from natural causes, and she didn't offer any information. Whenever I brought up the subject of her family, she just said, "They die a long time—no more talk about dying." I asked one of the other nurses about where Lanh came from and how she got a job as a nurse, knowing that most Vietnamese who worked there at the hospital did not have contact with the patients. Lanh was a medical student before her parents died. Most of the educated Vietnamese were schooled in the north, but there were a few who were college educated in Saigon or Hue.

The story was that some colonel at MACV vouched for Lanh after seeing her work triage for thirty-six hours non-stop on two A-teams at the Field Hospital in Nha Trang, and that wasn't her first triage. Lanh was a bright girl who everybody liked, so the hospital commander flew her down to Saigon and took her under his wing as a favor to the colonel.

Some of the other nurses came by to ask if I needed anything, and we shared idle chitchat. The doctors checked my progress pretty regularly. These visits were about as warm and personal as reveille. Lanh stopped by a few times each day— sometimes to change the dressing on my wound or to see if I was in pain. We made small talk, but mostly we made eye contact—though sometimes words did find their way past the obvious affection we had for each other. I liked listening to her, and her mouth moved funny when she talked.

"Why you smile—you happy?"

"I like the shape of your mouth when you talk."

She leaned over and placed a kiss on my lips, the likes of which I'd never known. I kissed women before, but no woman ever kissed me like that. Then she whispered, "We get you fixed up, okay? Then you go home. No more fight, no more Vietnam. I not can be with one GI too much. They say is not good."

"What do you say, Lanh?"

"Not understand, but my heart say not true."

"It's okay, Lanh. I understand. Just come see me when you can, okay?"

She smiled, and off she went. I'd never had a woman take the lead. Back in the Bronx, it was unheard of—but this was different. Lanh was special. I was sure that things like this happened in war. Who wouldn't be attracted to someone soft and warm in the midst of all that death? Love in war—it was common as the rain. Or so I'd heard. Hey, who cared? At least there was something else to think about instead of the war, and Lanh was something else to think about, all right. She was lovely, even in her fatigues. She wore her long, beautiful black hair up during working hours. Off duty, her hair was down to her waist—soft and silky. I never saw hair like that before. She was intoxicating.

Lanh began to spend more and more time helping me recover from my wound. The other patients and some of the staff started to see what was happening, and they probably thought it was cute or impossible. I'm sure they figured it was a sure bet that after I recovered, I'd be shipped stateside, and this little wartime fling would be just that, but Lanh and I were in love. It was something like nothing else I'd ever felt before. She took care of me, and I helped her with her English. We were taking care of each other. I didn't understand it all, but it felt good. She had my heart, and I wanted it that way.

One of the other patients had a guitar next to his bed. It was nothing fancy—one of those "Made in Vietnam" types. Then again, so was Lanh.

I had nothing better to do unless Lanh came to visit, so I asked the guy if I could borrow it for a while. It didn't sound that good, but it had six strings. I'd learned a few chords and some songs from a guy in high school. I kept learning songs mostly from other guys who played and from listening to the radio. I didn't read music or anything. I just picked it up by ear and eventually built up a bit of a repertoire. Back at the firebase, I played for the guys every now and then. We didn't get much entertainment out there, so anybody who could sing and play the guitar got an ego boost from a pretty damned attentive audience. It was a privilege to play for them—just ordinary guys living under extraordinary circumstances. Funny, but I never played for Lanh.

As I became able to move around, Lanh and I spent more and more time together. I bought her a few simple things from the PX, like makeup, perfume, lavender soap, and a radio with a tape player. She asked for nothing, but I wanted to give her everything. To us, the war was a million miles away. We stole every possible moment we could, and we didn't care about the consequences. We were inseparable. It wasn't often, but sometimes Lanh was able to get time alone for us in a room near radiology where the doctors would sack out after pulling an all-nighter. It was there that Lanh made love to me, and we professed our love for each other. Nothing I ever did before felt so right. We consumed each other's body and soul and exchanged the words, the kisses, and the touching that lovers do until we were set like mortar and stone. We exalted in this newfound oneness, sharing each other's bodies and solidifying ourselves as one. I'd said "I love you" before to other women without even knowing what it meant, but it took coming to this strange place, eleven thousand miles from Yonkers, to learn what "I love you" truly meant. When Lanh said "*em yeu anh*," which is I love you in Vietnamese, it resonated with the solemnity of prayer. I so wanted to belong to her. I began to set the wheels of my future in motion. I was going to ask Lanh to return to the states with me.

I went to the hospital commander to get permission to file the necessary paperwork. He tried to dissuade me from pursuing it further, but I think even he knew I wanted this more than anything. Finally, he gave me his blessing, wished me luck, and sent me to personnel to complete all the forms required to marry a Vietnamese national and bring her back to the United States. The military had to do a routine background check and a whole bunch of legal stuff to make sure she wasn't a Communist. Knowing the Army, I'd bet that something would go wrong. After going through miles of military red tape, I decided to go to the big PX in Long Binh to buy an engagement ring for Lanh.

During all the months I was in the hospital, I took no pay, so I had a bundle of cash waiting for me at the Finance Office. As I rode on the shuttle bus back to the hospital ward, I wondered how I was going to propose to her. Would she say yes? God, I hoped so. She never mentioned any living family, so it wasn't like she would be leaving anything or anyone behind. I had a million thoughts on how to propose to her but finally decided to put the ring in the top pocket of her uniform in her locker. I waited until all the nurses had changed into their scrubs, and then I made my way into the male-prohibited locker room. Opening the door of the locker, I noticed a picture of me taped to the inside of the locker door. She'd taken the picture when my wound was healing, and I was able to stand up.

There was a small straw bag at the bottom of the locker. I got curious and looked inside the bag. I wished I hadn't. There was a pair of black PJs in the bag, the kind worn by the Vietcong, and a Chinese Communist 9 mm pistol. This couldn't be. Could it? I felt a pit in my stomach, and I didn't know what to think. Just then, Lanh walked into the locker room.

"What you do in my locker?"

"I was leaving this for you," I said, showing her the ring.

"What is this, Lanh?" I showed her the bag with the black PJs and the pistol. Grabbing the bag from me, she started to cry.

"Talk to me, Lanh. What's happening here?"

"I hate Americans in my country, but I love you. You are good man. Go home now."

I slammed my hand against the locker door repeatedly.

"I wanted to bring you with me. That's what the ring is for, so we could get married. Now I find out that you're the enemy."

"I not enemy. No Vietcong. I love you"

"How can you love me when your people are killing my friends?"

"And your people kill my family. Mother, father, baby sister, all dead, kill by Americans."

"Lanh, I put in the paperwork and asked the Army for permission to marry you and bring you back to Yonkers with me. What am I supposed to do now?"

"No can marry you, Mac. Must go away. You go home," she said tearfully.

"But I love you, Lanh."

"I love you, too—must go now."

In what felt like the blink of an eye, the MPs burst into the locker room, locked and loaded their weapons on Lanh, and told her to drop to her knees with her hands behind her head. She pushed me out of the MPs' line of fire and reached inside her bag. The MPs opened fire on her with their shotguns. When they were sure she was dead, they asked if I was all right. I could only weep as I cradled her bloody, lifeless body, stroked her hair, and said over again, "*Em yeu anh rat nhieu*—I love you so very much."

Later, Military Intelligence came to the ward to question me. Lanh's whole family had been killed in a B-52 strike. I guessed that's what drove her to the other side. The MPs were tipped off during the routine background check. If I hadn't tried to marry her, she'd still be alive. The military was satisfied that I had no knowledge of Lanh's Vietcong activity. They just told me to forget everything and go home. Forget everything? The woman I loved had died in my arms. Go home? They could put me on a plane and send me back to Yonkers, but they couldn't make me forget Lanh, and they damn sure couldn't make me go home because the place didn't exist.

Nevertheless, my stateside orders were cut. I was scheduled to depart Cam Ranh Bay at 0600 hours to the place everyone else called home. All I did was go back to the place I ran away from—Yonkers. I had to blame someone for everything that happened, and God was first in the pecking order. If there was a God, then the blame was on Him. All I had now were cries of pain that resounded over and over again, so much so that it could frighten the wind. But a sea of tears was not deep enough to drown the sadness in my soul.

I boarded the freedom bird and headed back to the world, but emotionally I was adrift in a void that appeared out of nowhere with no boundaries, only endless space. Maybe the winds of change that carried the big silver bird away from Vietnam and everything I ever knew about it would be merciful and lose me somewhere between sunlight and shadows. I'd heard it said that time was a healer. Maybe so, but it'd be a patch job at best because my heart had already hardened, and it wouldn't surface again without extreme caution. Hyper-Vigilance became the fortress that protected me, and it was welcomed. I'd never felt the way I did about anyone before Lanh. After her death, survival came before sentimentality. I felt as if the guns had anesthetized my nerve endings. The only advice that was worth a damn came from the Chaplain, who said, "Don't try to make sense of something that makes no sense. Just accept it and move on."

At times it felt like the whole turn of events was a game of five-card stud. The cards were dealt within an acceptable range of fairness, but the queen of hearts threw in a wild card that I didn't expect. I often think of Lanh as a rose tangled in the thorns of this latest war-to-end-all-wars, who somehow got caught between barbed wire and claymore mines. For a brief moment amid the pounding of the guns, I allowed myself to believe in magic, and for as long as I live, I am left to remember it. So, thanks again, God—thanks for nothing!

Chapter 6: A Sort of Homecoming

Seattle-Tacoma Airport was pretty deserted when I got there after processing in from Vietnam. They put us through the normal hurry-up-and-wait routine that the military is known for, and so I just went along. I remembered something one of my pilots used to say: "You have to cooperate to graduate." It sounded good, but it translated into, "Screw it. Don't mean nothing." I was going back to the world to someplace the Army listed as my home. I left the place when I was sixteen because we were starving, and somebody had to put food on the table. My father—well, let's just say he decided to retire early and let public assistance take over. Except for an occasional poker game with my brother and some of his bookie friends, he just watched television, drank coffee, and smoked cigarettes all day, every day. My mother stood by idly. What else could she have done? She didn't pick her battles well. She only knew how to avoid them. I guess she stayed with him out of Christian obligation, but God never did anything to help her. If He did, I never saw it.

I stopped by two years ago to see my mother while I was on furlough before shipping out to Vietnam. I wanted to make sure she got to keep the allotment checks that I sent her and that they did not end up in my father's pocket. She'd get regular checks every month while I was in service. That way, at least, she wouldn't go hungry. Still, I worried about her. I actually worried about both of them. I used to wonder what they were having for dinner. Were they getting enough to eat? Did they have the clothes they needed? Maybe I shouldn't have cared about my father since he did nothing to help the situation, but I did. It was important to me that they were all right.

I left Yonkers to join the Army, so I could help take care of my family, even though I wasn't supposed to be the one doing that. I was a kid, and that job was for a grownup to do, but the grownup wasn't doing it.

I got off the plane at JFK International from Seattle-Tacoma Airport, and no sooner had I picked up my duffle bag when some guy with shoulder-length hair who looked like he needed a bath said, "Hey, how's it feel to be a baby killer?" I wanted to knock him on his butt, but I just moved on, hailed a taxi, and got into the back seat of the Checker with my gear.

"Where to, Sarge?" asked the driver.

"Just hop on the Parkway, head north, and get me out of here."

The driver looked like every other cabbie in New York City. He had a work shirt on with two top pockets and a newsboy's cap with his hack button pinned on the side. He tried to make small talk. "You just got back from overseas?"

"Yeah."

"Vietnam?"

"Uh-huh."

"How was it?"

"Well, I ain't afraid of hell anymore."

"That bad, huh?"

"Worse."

"Let me ask you something—do you think we belong over there?"

"I don't think anybody belongs over there, not even the Vietnamese."

I was dog-tired, and I really didn't feel like playing twenty questions.

"Listen, not to cut you short, but I need some shut-eye. Can you get me to Yonkers?"

"Sure, Sarge. No problem. I'll wake you when we get there."

As I slept, I dreamed about Lanh. I could see her long, flowing hair, and I could feel her soft cool breath on my face. I could hear her say what we said to each other so many times. *Em yeu anh rat nhieu—I love you so much.* Her mouth moved in that funny little way it always did when she spoke. She was wearing her fatigues. She always looked good in them, but she would have looked stunning in a burlap sack. God, she was so beautiful. Hers was not a look of innocence. It was more a look of quiet strength with a topping of loyalty, and it was loyalty that got her killed. Her love ran deep enough to sacrifice herself for me. Could anyone have loved someone more? Christian scriptures teach that *greater love has no one than this, that one lay down his life for his friends.* Change the gender in the quote, and that's exactly what Lanh did. It goes without saying that her young life ended tragically. The sadness of losing her would always haunt me in ways that no one would ever comprehend. She had nothing, and she gave me everything. I had everything and gave her nothing except my heart—and it still belonged to her.

"OK, Sarge. Up and at 'em. We're here in downtown Yonkers. What street do you want?"

"Just drop me at the corner of Smith Street and Yonkers Avenue."

"Okay, the corner it is. Your folks know you're coming?"

"Nobody knows. Okay, this is good. What do I owe you?"

"Ah, the meter says thirteen fifty, but just give me ten bucks—servicemen's discount."

"Here's twenty. Thanks for the ride."

"Anytime, Sarge, and welcome home."

"Yeah, thanks."

I grabbed my gear out of the Checker and started walking up Smith Street. Passing Dee's Coffee Shop brought back the memory of my first banana split when Dee's wife, Linda, put three extra cherries on it, and I thought I was in Heaven. The coffee shop was still there and as busy as Macy's at Christmas. I stopped in to see if anybody I knew was hanging out there, and sure enough, there was my old flame Susan working behind the counter. Seeing her again brought back memories—some good, some not so good. There were the "holding hands across the table" memories, like when she promised to wait for me until I got back from Vietnam, and then there was the "I want to move on" memory when I was home on furlough. It hurt at the time when Susan mailed me the paper bullet, but I kind of understood she had plans that didn't include going to my funeral. My mom liked her but didn't think she was the one for me.

"Ray, I'm so glad you're home."

"Thanks, Susan."

"Your mom told me you got wounded. Are you okay?"

"Yeah, I'm all right. I took a bit of shrapnel in my right leg, but it healed well."

"I'm glad to hear that, Ray. Your mom said that you met a girl over there and that she was killed."

"I really don't want to talk about it, Susan. Done is done, and talking won't bring her back."

"I'm sorry, Ray. It sounds like you loved her very much."

"Yeah, I did."

"Maybe if I didn't break it off, you wouldn't have met, and she'd still be alive."

"Don't go blaming yourself because it's not about you."

"Can you forgive me for breaking it off, Ray?"

"There's nothing to forgive. You had other plans, and I was still in the army. Things happen for a reason, Susan. It's nobody's fault, just circumstances."

"Well, my plans didn't quite work out, as you can see. I'm working here and going to night school to be a teacher, and that's pretty much it. What about you, Ray? Got any plans yet?"

"Nothing past today. I don't want to think that far ahead."

"Do you think we could go out sometime, Ray?"

"I don't know, Susan. I don't think my heart would be in it. Right now, I just need some time to myself to try and figure things out. Beyond that, I haven't got a clue."

"Well, you can find me here if you want some company or anything."

"Thanks, Susan. I think I'm just going to fly solo for a while."

I saw my friend, Benny, just outside the coffee shop. We'd been friends since grade school. He was a good guy, and he played good handball. He saw me and waved me over.

"Yo, Ray!"

"Hey, Benny. How's your pecker hanging?"

"Cocked and ready to fire, like always."

"Where's numb nuts? Where's Petey?"

"He's in the deli. He'll be out in a minute. So, are you back for good? How does it feel to be home?"

"Home? Where's that, Benny?"

"Whaddya mean *where's that?* It's here, Smith Street, Yonkers."

"Benny, if I had a farm on Smith Street and a home in Hell, I'd sell my farm and go home. This isn't home. It's just someplace, somewhere on the map."

Petey came out of the deli with a hero sandwich that had to be a foot and a half long.

"Guess you're hungry, huh, numbnuts?"

"Hey, shithead, you're home! 'Bout freakin' time."

"Yeah, I figured you missed me. You gonna eat that whole thing by yourself, you pig?"

"Probably, unless you guys wanna help me eat it. It's good to see you, Ray. Heard you got wounded—you okay?"

"Thanks, Petey. Yeah, I'm all right."

"Does it hurt?"

"Sometimes. Listen, you guys wanna have a quick game of handball?"

"I'm always up for a game," Petey said.

"Me too," Benny resounded.

We crossed the street, laughing and chowing down on Petey's hero sandwich just like we did when we were kids. Benny slammed the ball up against the brick firehouse wall, and then Petey came back and hit it high so I could send it sailing to the wall from the back fence of the schoolyard. For a moment, it was 1960, when we were ten years old, playing handball and listening to Gene Chandler sing "Duke of Earl" on a transistor radio that hung from a door handle on the fire engine. It wasn't perfect, but it was good. Maybe Benny was right. This was home—but it was his home, not mine—not anymore.

I finally reached the apartment building where my parents lived. It was old, built in the 1900s, but it was nice and clean. Mary McGovern was out front sweeping the stoop and sidewalk that bordered the two-story walkup. She and her family lived next door to my parents. Mary and "Big Jim" McGovern came to America from Ireland in the 1930s and moved into the building in 1949, just two months before my parents did. Her son, Brian, and I were friends growing up. He was killed somewhere in the Mekong Delta the year before while I was still in the country. I could see the sadness on her face as I came closer to the building. In a brogue that was as thick as molasses, I heard her shout up toward my mother's bedroom window, "Mary! Mary! Raymond's home!" My mother looked out the window to see, and then she hurried downstairs.

Her eyes filled with tears, and she threw her arms around me, saying my name over and over in her Scottish burr. I glanced over at Mary McGovern as I hugged my mother. She held her hands over her face. Thoughts of the son who never came home must've overwhelmed her when she saw us. I called her name and waved her over. With one arm around her and the other around my mom, I held them both close as they thanked Jesus, Mary, and Joseph for bringing me back safe in the same familiar brogue and burr that I'd heard all my life.

As I entered the apartment, my dad was in the same position he was when I left: watching television, drinking coffee, and smoking cigarettes. He turned toward me in his chair and then went back to watching television. Guess I wasn't gone long enough. I sat in the kitchen with my mom. She filled me in as to what was going on in the family and the neighborhood. It seems my never-do-well brother has had more than a few brushes with the law. My father overlooked it as long as my brother brought home the cash. And why wouldn't he? Money has no conscience.

I'd have thought that someone who served in the military would at least be glad to see his son returning home safely. Dad used to be an upright, honest man. He came to this country as a young boy with strict traditional parents. My grandmother was tough but fair, and she taught her children to be honest, decent people. My father was a street vendor in Manhattan, selling hot dogs, pretzels, and candy apples. He brought home good money until he lost his vendor's permit somehow. I never knew the reason, but he didn't seem to care about anything after that—not even his youngest son returning home from the war. I got up from the table and walked into the living room. I thought my father had some explaining to do, so I was pretty much picking a fight and wishing he would take a swing at me so that I'd have a reason to swing back.

"Does it even matter to you that I'm alive? You know I got wounded in combat."

"Yeah, I know. What do you want me to say?"

"How about welcome home, son—are you okay? Does it hurt where you got hit?"

"What for? You're standing here, aren't you? You want me to fuss over you like your mother does?"

"Yeah, maybe a little. Would it kill you?"

"No, but my father never fussed over me."

"And look what happened. You quit working years ago, and I joined the Army just to send money home so that none of you would starve."

"You sent the money home to your mother, not me."

"Yeah, because you would've kept it for yourself. She would've never seen a penny."

"As long as I'm head of this family, I decide what gets done and who does it."

"You gave up that right years ago. Mom and I are the only ones who have done anything to keep this family alive."

"Yeah, what about your brother?"

"You mean, your son, if you call running numbers making a living. Looks like I came back to the wrong house because the father I knew used to be an honest man."

"Well, I carried all of you long enough. Now you can carry me."

"Don't count on it. I'm through taking care of you. Mom's my only concern."

"Oh yeah? Go ahead and take her with you. She don't do nothing for me anyway except cook."

"Well, then, stock up on canned food because she's through being your slave."

He turned away from me, waving his hand in dismissal.

"Come on, Ma. Pack some things, and I'll bring you to Aunt Jane's."

"I can't, Raymond. My place is here."

"He doesn't even care about you."

"But I have to care for him. He's my husband."

"He wouldn't do the same for you."

"Maybe not, but he has no one else to care for him."

"He has his thieving son."

"You mean your brother."

"No, Mom, his son—he's no brother of mine."

"Yes, he is, and he's my son too, and don't you ever say he's not your brother. I gave life to both of you. This is your family, good or bad, and you have to take the good with the bad. It broke my heart to see you go into the Army just to send money home. I wish your brother were like you, but he's like your father."

"I know, but he's older. Isn't he supposed to help the family too? Come on, Ma. I almost got killed trying to keep this family alive."

"There's nothing nobler than a boy who takes on a man's job. You did what you thought had to be done, and I'm proud of you for it. Now go see your friends and tell me about Lanh sometime. I'm so sorry for you, son. She sounded like a lovely girl."

Lanh was a lovely girl, and no woman I ever met could even so much as pack her lunch. I left the house and called a cab from the phone booth in the coffee shop to take me over to Fort Hamilton for processing out of the Army. Mine and Susan's initials were still on the wooden platform under the telephone after all this time. I carved them into the wood with a ballpoint pen. Well, at least something was kept. It was almost a year after Susan, and I broke up before I met Lanh. I didn't want to take a walk down memory lane with Susan, and I really wasn't brushing her off. I guess I just needed one more reason to dislike this sort of homecoming. I wasn't expecting a parade or anything, but no one talked to me in the coffee shop except Susan. Maybe they just didn't know what to say.

The news reports we heard on AFVN radio talked about riots and anti-war protestors, so I figured it was a safe bet that the welcome home would be lukewarm at best. There were no conquerors, but there were heroes—lots of them. Ordinary people living and dying under extraordinary circumstances and hoping they would make it home. I wanted to go back to Nam, but the Army would never let that happen. I was put on a plane and sent back to somewhere I didn't want to be. I knew the faces of everybody on the Island, every nook and cranny. It was good to see my mom, Susan, and the guys too. I wanted out of here, but I had nowhere else to go. The taxi came. I jumped in and headed for Fort Hamilton in Brooklyn. I collected my back pay and processed out of military service. I didn't know what to do or where I was going after the Army, so I did whatever came along, and for a while, God stayed out of the way.

Chapter 7: The Christmas Child

As things would have it, God had been listening to my silent prayers, and He stayed the hell out of my way. I thought about everything that happened in Vietnam and after I came back. For the life of me, God never cut me one damn bit of slack. Maybe He forgot about me years ago when I failed to do some church thing and considered me a lost cause. Well, the feeling was mutual, so I figured that made us even. What the hell did God ever do except kick my ass from one side of the planet to the other? I went hungry as a child, and He didn't send any food. My mother was sick her whole life, and He didn't seem to care about her. She went to church every single day and said a Novena every week, yet God didn't bring any relief from the suffering she endured. What kind of God was He? I didn't have a clue, and I didn't say prayers to Him or any Saint anymore. That would make about as much sense as pissing in the wind.

Nothing is free in this life, not even dreams—and even when they come true, there's a price to be paid. My dream came in the form of a child—a beautiful little girl with honey hair, a pug nose, and the most beautiful blue eyes I ever saw. As any parent knows, having a child costs big time. Beyond prenatal costs, delivery costs, postnatal costs, and every doctor bill imaginable, children still need things constantly, and that goes with the turf.

As a parent, I wanted everything good for my child—nothing but the best—but the best costs money. Hell, even the worst costs money. Yet, it was worth it, especially when I looked into Emily's eyes and saw so much promise, so many possibilities. Having a child changed me greatly, and I was in need of change. There are things I did that I normally wouldn't have done if I didn't have a child. Those occasions and things came along more often than I was ready for.

I met Ellen McGuiness when I was twenty years old and in college after military service. I was studying graphic design, and she, like all good Irish Catholic girls, took the more practical approach, which in this case was nursing. We had lunch in the cafeteria one day, and I asked her to the movies on a Saturday. She seemed nice enough, and we were attracted to each other. There's probably an exception to the rule somewhere, but generally speaking, Irish Catholic girls don't put out, at least not without a ring, and not even then most times.

As it goes with the natural order of things, I proposed to Ellen and gave her an engagement ring, but she still wouldn't have sex out of wedlock. We got married, and Emily was conceived nine months to the day. I started calling Ellen "one-shot" McGuiness after that. Somebody once told me that Irish

Catholic girls get pregnant if you smile at them. There may be some truth to that. We started fighting about money. No surprise there since that is common with newlyweds; however, after two years of bickering and screaming at each other, we decided to call it quits—no sense beating a dead mule. We didn't love each other. Hell, we didn't even like each other. I think we were in lust with each other, but that only goes so far when the rest of your days are fraught with arguments. Emily was important to both of us, so much so that we agreed she didn't deserve to watch us fight all the time. No one tried to talk us out of divorce, and we knew it was the only thing to do. For Emily's sake, it was for the best. Ellen and I divorced when Emily was just three years old.

We were far too young to marry when we did, and we kept it going after Emily was born, but it seemed that we both did our level best to piss each other off. Eventually, too much was said and done to get past the hurt. Our intentions were good, but we just couldn't figure out how to make it work. We had almost no support from our families, so in due course, the happily ever after we always talked about came crashing down.

After the divorce, another court battle ensued to determine when I was allowed to see Emily. A total stranger was going to decide when I could be with my daughter. Well, that surely qualified as bullshit to me, and I expressed that sentiment in the courtroom, which did not please the judge, to say the least. It was more or less characteristic of Ray MacDonald to say and do the wrong thing at the wrong time. The court ordered that I pay seventeen percent of my income for child support and granted visitation rights with Emily every Saturday from ten in the morning until six in the eve. This gave me eight hours one day a week to be a father. I tried hard to be a good father to Emily, trying to make up for the time I wasn't with her. She was in my thoughts constantly, and I kept thinking of ways I could be a better father and make the time I had with her as good as I could be. I tried to do fun things with her. We went to the park a lot. I even played in the sandbox with her. Sometimes we took in a movie, especially in the hot weather. There was a small amusement park in Cross County Shopping Center in Yonkers, not too far from Yonkers. We went there on Saturdays in the nice weather.

As Emily got older, the court and her mother allowed her to sleep over once or twice a month. It was great. I loved having her around. I didn't earn much money, but we managed to have fun. I worried about money a lot, and I didn't have a car, so I had to work locally, and the jobs didn't pay very well. I was able to find regular work plus a part-time job without either of them cutting into my time with Emily. My jobs were nearby, so I was able to walk or take a bus to work.

It didn't always work out, but sometimes I was able to take a course here and there at a local college, but every day was a financial struggle. I always had to make sure I had lunch money and taxi money for Emily when she started school. She was so good-natured. She never asked for much of anything. I felt so lucky to have a child like her. I saw lots of kids in the supermarket screaming their heads off, with their mothers smacking them for every tear they shed. I could never hit Emily. I might think it, but I could never lay a hand on her.

My brother had the role of being the family criminal, and since I didn't follow in his footsteps, I wasn't likely to do anything illegal, but I'd have done almost anything to turn a buck. Like anyone else, I did whatever I had to do to make a living. That meant washing dishes, picking up garbage, and driving a taxi. I had a child to take care of, and that meant I'd do whatever, even if it meant wearing a tie. So far, I'd been pretty lucky. If I lost a job, I'd find another in a day or so.

When I was a kid, it was easy to get money. I'd walk up and down Yonkers Avenue and stop in every store on the way to see if anybody needed help doing anything. Somebody always needed help with something. The first stop was the Blarney Rose Bar and Grill. Rosie McDonough owned the place by herself, and she was good for a few bucks to take the boxes of empty beer bottles outside for the beer truck to collect.

Next, I'd hit up old Ben Granat at the candy store. I could make two dollars loading up the soda case, and on Sunday, I'd make a dollar helping him bring the papers inside the store. It was easy to make a buck then. Now it took twice the effort to make half as much.

I picked up a few bucks helping a Ukrainian guy install stained glass windows in a Russian Orthodox Church in New Jersey. It was enough to pay this week's child support and some carry-over money until the next job. It wasn't the kind of job where I needed a Ph.D—only a strong back. The windows were really beautiful. I could see that the guy must've spent hours on the figures alone. The detail in the faces was something to see. This guy was a real artist, but I didn't have time to spend admiring somebody's artwork. I needed to make money, but I could never seem to find a job that could pay me enough. Often, I'd see people in their jobs and think to myself, "I could do just as good a job as they can," but every time I went for a job I really wanted, I'd always get turned down for one reason or another. Either I wasn't qualified, or the job was too far away to use the bus or walk. I'd like to get myself a good decent paying job with benefits, but they wanted college degrees for jobs like that. With only a few courses under my belt, I didn't stand a chance.

For the past few months, I worked for a roofing company down the road. Mostly I picked up the scraps of shingles that the roofers threw down. It didn't pay great, but for six bucks an hour, I'd pick up shingles and any other junk they'd throw off the roof. Sometimes I got up on the roof to help the roofers lay down new shingles and got paid three dollars an hour extra. After doing the roofing thing all day, I drove a taxi at night and on weekends. I kept Monday and Wednesday open in case I was able to take another course at the college.

Saturday was reserved for Emily alone. I didn't do anything without her on that day. If she spent the night, we'd usually make a big bowl of popcorn and watch "The Love Boat" on television. One of the characters, Vicki, was a young girl and the Captain's daughter. Emily really liked her. When she watched the program, she'd always say, "Boy, Vicki is so lucky. She gets to live on a boat and stuff." Yeah, she was lucky, and so was everyone on the boat, but that's Hollywood, and Hollywood doesn't happen in Yonkers. All we had were boats and fish and tourists in the summer with their tourist money. They always seemed to have an endless supply of it.

During the summer, I helped out on the touring boats on Sundays. Tips were usually good, and the number of customers per excursion paid the crew. On a good day, each of us on the crew could make anywhere from fifty to a hundred bucks. If I had made that much, I wouldn't have had to drive the cab on that Sunday night. Working the boat was hard and I was always beat by day's end.

I got laid off from roofing when it was slow, so I got work at a diner washing dishes and helping out with the cooking. The diner was okay, but it certainly was not my dream job. I took home the leftover roast beef or Virginia Ham to my mom. She really enjoyed it and didn't have it very often.

Those kinds of fatty meats really weren't good for her, with being sick most of her life in one form or another. She'd been born with scarlet fever, and back then, most children died from it. It left her somewhat slow, so she never finished school. She could read and write a little, but she couldn't tell time or the difference between ten and twenty-dollar bills. I was amazed by how she got along all these years.

Talk about going from bad to worse. I just got off the phone with Emily's mother. All I heard was, "What are you going to do about Christmas? Are you going to give me some support this week?" Then, like always, an argument ensued. I didn't know how, but I was once married to that woman. I must've been out of my mind, but the holidays were getting close, and I got the worst news yet. Three weeks before Christmas and I got laid off from the diner. It's not like I was making a fortune, but the boss said he couldn't afford to keep me. He really felt bad, so he gave me a few bucks extra in my pay envelope and some food. I appreciated it, but he didn't feel half as bad as I did. What was I going to do about Christmas for Emily? She hadn't asked for anything, but I couldn't just forget about Christmas. I didn't have a lot of money saved, only forty bucks at home. How was I going to explain this to Ellen? It'd be better if I didn't.

I had to get work damn quick, but the only jobs open were in retail. If I took a job there, I'd have to work every Saturday, and I wouldn't get to see Emily on the one visitation day I had. If Ellen had been more agreeable, I could have switched my visitation day to Sunday, and finding a job might be easier. But Sunday was a family day with Ellen, her new husband, and his children. Funny how there was no family day when we were married.

My old friend, Joe Chesler, a retired police officer, called and asked me to help him collect donations pledged by local merchants for the Pelham Police Department's Christmas Fund. I wasn't doing anything, and he said he'd drive me to look for work if I helped him, so I figured why not. I picked up donations mostly from small businesses and doctors' offices in the New Rochelle and Pelham area, both of which were a stone's throw from Yonkers.

Around mid-day, I stopped to pick up a donation at the Pelham Limousine Service. I couldn't afford to live in Pelham, but it was really nice to visit. Joe waited in the car as the owner and I had small talk. She waived to Joe through the window and wrote the check for the donation.

"Are you a police officer?" she asked.

"No, ma'am. Just giving Joe a hand. I'm actually looking for work."

"Do you have a chauffeur's license?"

"I sure do."

"If you're interested, I could use another driver if you don't mind working at night."

"Not at all, but I haven't chauffeured anyone since I drove for a colonel when I was in the Army stationed at the Pentagon."

"You'll do fine. Can you start tonight?"

"Yes."

"Good. You'll need a dark suit, white shirt, and tie, and get a good, clean haircut."

"Thanks, I really appreciate the work."

"You're welcome. Now be nice to the client, open the door, say "yes ma'am" and "yes sir", and be on time. If you do all that, your tips will be good, and eventually, I'll give you more select calls. Are we clear?"

"Yes, ma'am. It sounds fine to me. I'll see you tonight."

Me? Driving a limousine? No one is going to believe this—hell; I didn't even believe it.

I spent twenty of the forty bucks I had to get a haircut and a new shirt and tie. Thank God I already had a black suit. I picked it up last year at the Salvation Army store for twenty-five dollars in case there was a wedding or a funeral. Weddings and funerals are not much different. My mom was right.

Mom said she'd pray that I'd do all right with the limousine. I guess a prayer from my mother's mouth to God's ears wouldn't hurt. I was still pissed off at God, but for Emily's sake and out of respect for my mother, I said a prayer of my own:

"God, if you're there and if you can hear me, how about doing me a solid? I'm doing the best I can, and I keep falling flat on my face. So, if you wouldn't mind, how about a little miracle or just make the ground a little softer."

I took a cab to the limousine company, and I had a call within twenty minutes. This was a cakewalk—a trip to LaGuardia Airport. I got my client there in nineteen minutes. He promised a twenty-dollar tip if I got him there within twenty minutes. The rest of the evening was great. I made three more airport trips and went home with a hundred twenty-five in salary and eighty dollars in tips. For six hours of work, it's the fastest two hundred and five I've ever made. I don't know. Is it a miracle, or is it just dumb luck? I'd been crashing my cymbals out there for five years, trying to figure out how to get ahead and make a decent living without doing something illegal. All I knew was something clicked, and I wasn't about to start asking too many questions.

I continued to drive the limousine almost every night and sometimes during the day. I earned between hundred seventy-five and three hundred dollars per shift. I socked away as much money as I could in case the job ended after Christmas. That way, at least I'd have a little bit of a cash cushion to tie me over until the next job. Maybe I could make driving the limousine my next job. It sure beats getting filthy doing odd jobs. It was clean, the people were nice, and it was the best money I ever made. So, I thought I'd keep this gig until I got a college degree, and then I could get a better job with some benefits. I thought, "Yes, this is my ticket to the bigs."

Now that I had a few bucks in my pocket, where the hell was I going to find someplace open to get Emily's presents on Christmas Eve? Holy shit! Toys "R" Us is open till midnight! They had everything from toys to children's books to children's clothes. I started picking out some toys for Emily. She liked this doll called "Whoopsie" and the "Snoopy Snow

Cone Machine." She liked books, and I found one about Unicorns that I thought she'd like. I picked out some stocking stuffer things like "Strawberry Shortcake" stickers and some "Smurf" trinkets and gadgets.

They had some cute outfits for little girls and I found two in Emily's size. This was good—hell, it might even impress Ellen that I remembered to get clothes for Emily. I didn't care if I impressed her. I just didn't want to fight over money anymore. I wanted to give Emily a good Christmas this year. As far as next Christmas, well, I'll jump off that bridge when I get to it.

As I looked back over the past few weeks, it was hard to believe everything that had happened. I was grateful for how everything turned out, but all this hadn't just fallen out of a tree. Had I just gotten lucky, or was I finally in the right place at the right time? Maybe it was all just coincidence. I heard that it was God's way of being anonymous—hmm.

Chapter 8: Folky

The limousine gig turned out to be a real lifesaver and the best-paying job I'd had since I got out of the service. After doing it for two years, I had it down to a science. My shift allowed me to spend good quality time with my daughter, Emily, and I even continued with college. Although I hadn't declared a major yet, I only needed another eighteen credits to earn my degree. I'd have to think about declaring a major at some point, but for now, I just continued to march.

Lately, I've been playing my guitar more, probably because I spend so much time by myself. I went to listen to some of the local musicians play at tavern restaurants, and some of these guys were pretty good. Some performers worked as a duo, like "Two Bits." Those guys were a riot, as well as being good musicians. They had a slogan on their banner that said, "Two Bits—the only pair that equals a quarter." They were real cutups. Other local duos like "Two's Company" played just about everywhere, but probably the most successful local duo was "Twisted Pair." Those guys could draw a crowd week after week to the same place, and the audience couldn't get enough of them. They were pretty decent guys who knew how to work the crowd. Some of the material they played was kind of hokey and bubble gummy, but who am I to judge? They had standing good paying gigs, and they were having a ball. Now, that was a great way to waste a Saturday night and make side money too.

I learned to play guitar while I was still in high school. I picked up a few songs and got pretty good at it. Most of the stuff I played was considered folk rock, but I learned a few R&B tunes in Vietnam from the bloods. Motown was always good to put a smile on our faces. A Smokey Robinson, Stevie Wonder, or Marvin Gaye tune always hit home for the bloods—and me too. The guys didn't care that I was white and played R&B. All they cared about was that it connected them to home. We were brothers, all of us. The only thing between us was air and very little of that. The bloods always appreciated the music when I played for them. They were my family, and I loved every one of them.

When I came back stateside, I heard some guy in a music store play the most beautiful-sounding guitar I'd ever heard. When I asked about it, he said it was a D-28 Martin. Damn, that guitar sounded great. The only problem was that they weren't cheap. In 1973, they cost about five hundred dollars and as a soldier I only made three-fifty a month, so Martin would have to wait for another time, which didn't come until five years after my divorce from Ellen. She got all the marital assets, so all I had was my duffel bag full of clothes and a beat-up Yamaha guitar. It sounded all right, but I could never forget the sound of that Martin. Eventually, after driving the limousine for a while, I was able to buy the D-28 Martin that I loved so much. It was like I rediscovered music all over again. I'd played a little here and there over the years, but the Martin just made me want to play everywhere to anyone who would listen. The music I played was powerful, and it took me anywhere I wanted to be. The Martin made getting there that much sweeter.

I started to hang out in music stores more often. I was trying to bump elbows with other musicians, figuring I could get a handle on some paying gigs. We'd talk, and they'd give me the names of good places to play where the gig would pay a decent buck. You'd play the standard four hours and forty-five minutes on, fifteen minutes off schedule. It really wasn't hard to do if you had enough songs with enough variety in your repertoire. Mine was pretty good. I knew songs from the 1950s through the present. I could play pretty much anything from Folk to Country to Rock to R&B to Latin, and I had every song down pat by heart. Some performers still used sheet music while performing. I never subscribed to that because part of being the performer was memorizing the songs, but hey, everybody to their own. I was only trying to make extra money and have fun—and meet women.

Getting the gig was sometimes more work than playing the gig itself. Most people thought that playing music in public was all fun and games. The only fun part was playing for the audience and getting the applause. It was great, but it only lasted a bit while you were performing. Women wanted to ride your coattails because they thought it was exciting to hang out with a musician, but they didn't see the big picture.

You had to set up your gigs, practice, learn new songs, and make sure your gear was up to date and working properly. Beyond that, you were on the phone with tightwad club owners during the day who tried to get blood from a rock. They wanted you to play a four-hour gig for meager wages. Basically, what they wanted was entertainment for nothing. The club owners thought they were doing you a favor by giving you exposure to play in their club. They gave you the routine that "some A&R man from a major record label" was going to discover you in their club and make you a star, so you owed them. Things like that happened sometimes, but mostly you just made a few dollars, met some people and played superstar for a few hours. It allowed you to be somebody else for a little while. For a few hours, I wouldn't be Ray MacDonald, a schlep from the Bronx or a Vietnam veteran. I was a musician—a minstrel for hire—and that was a nice place to be, even in this little corner of the galaxy called Yonkers.

I made a new friend when Pete Stevens and I were both booked for the same gig at Beau Brummel's in New Rochelle. Double booking was common with club owners. I arrived at the gig before he did, and I was already set up. Pete was a regular performer there, and the rule was the steady guy gets the gig. But he didn't take it. Instead, he gave it to me, which was pretty decent of him. So, he sat back and became part of the audience. He applauded after each song, and the audience followed suit. This, of course, led to my credibility, not to mention my confidence as a performer. Later in the evening, I invited him up to play a couple of songs with me, and it was like magic.

His harmonies were as good as the Bee Gees—clear, clean, and tight. He turned out to be a good friend, which didn't always happen among musicians because there's always the competition thing going on.

Pete's musical style and mine were very different, so the normal backbiting musician nonsense didn't happen between us. For that and for his kindness, I was grateful. Pete and I got together from time to time, trying out new material and trading notes about club owners and other musicians. He had a small recording studio in his garage. We used to make demo tapes to copyright our original songs before they were sent to publishers. We were hoping to get that big break into the record industry, sometimes called "The Great Gig in the Sky," which was named after a Pink Floyd tune. We were trying to get to "the bigs" like everybody else, but mostly we were dreamers. I got a call about a gig from Pete one day. He was playing at a restaurant right on City Island called the Seascape. He got a standing gig playing at a place up in Westchester, and he thought I'd be interested in sharing the gig at the restaurant with him.

"Listen," he told me. "I got a new standing gig at the Lake Isle Country Club on Friday evenings, so the Fridays at the Seascape are yours if you want it. All you have to do is audition for Tommy, the manager. It's a steady gig every Friday night, and I play Saturday night. It runs from eight o'clock until midnight, and it goes from May through November. The pay is really good—dollars per night plus tips."

"Sounds great."

"Yeah, and you get free dinner too. And Ray, the food is fabulous."

"Okay, so where do I sign up?"

"I'll give Tommy a call and set up an audition. You'll do great."

"Thanks so much, Pete. I hope I can return the favor someday."

"I know you will. Good luck! Talk to you soon."

The Seascape Restaurant had been in business since about 1903. It was a nice place with great food, the kind of place you'd take a date if you wanted to impress her. And speaking of women, one of the benefits of being a musician was that you constantly met women. Ask any musician why they took up an instrument, and the reason was always the same—to meet girls. I guess women are attracted to the artistic types.

I arrived at the audition that Pete had set up for me at the Seascape. In two words, Tommy, the manager, was "very Italian." He had so many hand gestures that there was probably a tutorial called "Italian Hand Gestures 101". He was also very verbal and loud, and he had no problem using expletives when he addressed the kitchen staff. We talked for a bit, and then he asked me to play a few songs.

"What would you like to hear, Tommy?"

"I dunno; any freakin' thing. Just play somethin' good. Just don't play that 'Feelin' Groovy' bullshit. The last guy who played it, I threw 'em out on his ass. How's about playin' that wreck of the Edward so-and-so song?"

"You mean 'The Wreck of the Edmund Fitzgerald?'"

"Yeah, yeah, dats da one. Play dat, and ya gotta job. If ya stink at it, ya outta here."

This was going to be a walk in the park. The guy who wrote that song was my favorite singer-songwriter, Gordon Lightfoot. I'd listened to his songs since before Nam, and I probably had most of them memorized. I started the song out slow, lightly strumming the brand new Martin's silk and steel strings with a thin flat-pick using a Travis-style strum. The words took on a life of their own as I started to sing the tale of the ore carrier that sunk in Lake Superior in 1975.

"Dat was good, kid. Ya' got any more sea songs? This is a seafood restaurant ya know?"

"Yeah, I have a couple more."

I played another Gordon Lightfoot tune called "Christian Island". It was a smooth, laid-back, ballad-like song about spending a perfectly good day just sailing. For my last nautical song, I played an old Roger Whitaker song called "The River Lady". It was an up-tempo tribute to a riverboat about to be taken out of service.

"Hey kid, you know any Puerto Rican stuff? We get a lot of 'em down here on da weekends."

"I know a few Latino songs, if that's what you mean."

"Yeah, like dat, and hows about dat me and Julio schoolyard song?"

"Sure, I know that."

"Yeah, play dat one."

I started with a Latin strum, and the chorus flowed perfectly.

"Ya know, kid, Pete was right. You play real good. Okay, you come in Friday night and be ready to play by eight o'clock. No drinkin' and no screwin' around with waitresses while ya workin'. Ya get a hundred dollars a night plus tips, so don't f'get to put a brandy snifter out front, or ya' ain't gonna get shit. I expect ya' to entertain the customers in the lounge before dey go to dinner, so dat when dey finish eatin', dey come back to da lounge to hear more. Got it, folky?"

"Yes, sir. Folky?"

"Yeah, folky. And don't call me sir. I work for a living. Call me Tommy. Okay, now ya have dinner on da house between seven and eight o'clock. Dats before you start or on your break between nine and ten o'clock. Ya on forty-five and off fifteen, got it? And ya see Reuben at the bar when ya done so you can get paid. Dems da rules. Any questions?"

"No."

"Good, and make sure ya dress nice, eh? No jeans or cutoffs."

"Right, Tommy. See you on Friday. Thanks."

"Sure, kid, and say hi to Pete. You should thank him, too."

Tommy wasn't lying. Pete handed me the gig, and I needed it for lots of reasons. I showed up that first Friday night a little nervous but feeling confident. My setup was done in a matter of minutes, not forgetting the brandy snifter that Tommy mentioned. I was quick to christen the brandy snifter with two dollar bills and a prayer to Our Lady of Folksingers. I hadn't performed in a few months, so I'd started out with the moderate up-tempo "Back in the High Life" by Steve Winwood. It was as familiar as putting on my socks, and the audience responded well to it. I played it safe for the first set, so I could drop my musical anchor and not stray too far from the genre of songs that I was used to playing. I finished my first set successfully, wiped the sweat off the Martin, and took a break. The cocktail waitress brought me a glass of iced water, and it went down nice and easy, just like the set. Tommy stopped over with a few words of encouragement, which was really friendly ball-breaking. Something like, "Ya did okay, kid. Now play somethin' good, eh?" From him, that was a rave. I had fun and made money, and that was good enough.

The first season came and went, and I did well enough that Tommy asked me to come back for another season. I liked the place. I earned about hundred and fifty every Friday, including tips. That extra six hundred a month really helped out a lot. Making money from playing music had a sweeter taste than getting paid for driving a limousine. I was paid for the gig, but I also got recognition as an entertainer. I was a working musician, and I can't begin to tell you how good that felt. I could finally afford things for Emily that I never could before, and as long as I kept that up, Ellen didn't hassle me. Emily had started coming with me to my gigs every now and then. It was a late night for her, staying up until midnight, but she loved to watch me sing and play the guitar. Emily had her own favorite songs that she would ask me to play. She thought the singer Paul Young was "hot," and she asked me to learn one of his songs called "Every Time You Go Away." It was written by Darryl Hall, and I learned it pretty well so I could play it for her. When Emily wasn't watching me perform or playing video games, she was hanging out with Melissa, who managed the gift shop. She painted Emily's name on a piggy bank and gave it to her. She gave me a real good price on a Cabbage Patch Doll for Emily as well. It was sixty-five dollars, but I didn't care. Emily had fun, I made money, and we were together.

My father died when Emily was about five years old. Sometime before he died, he taught her to play cards, especially poker. What possessed him to do that was beyond me, but it was good that he cared about her enough to spend time with her. It was more than he gave me, which didn't equal much.

One Friday evening, in particular, it was kind of slow, so I played mostly laid-back folksy stuff. Sometimes Emily brought a deck of cards with her and played solitaire. Tommy came into the lounge and sat down at the table with Emily. He liked Emily. She got all the Shirley Temples she could drink and about a half dozen cherries in each one. All of eight years old, Emily dealt out a poker hand to Tommy and herself. They agreed on high-stakes poker—twenty-five cents a game. I hoped she didn't lose because she didn't have any money.

"Ya got anything good in dat hand, kid?"

"I'm not telling you."

"Awright, gimme tree cards."

"Dealer takes two."

"Ah, so all ya need is two?"

"Maybe—"

"Gotcha, kid. I got two pair. Whaddya got?"

"Three aces. I win!"

"Jesus, Ray, whaddya bringin' here, five-year-old card sharks?

I laughed like hell. My father was a bit of a card shark, and I guess he imparted his card skills to his granddaughter.

"Geesh, it's freakin' embarrassing gettin' beat by a kid."

"I'm not a kid. I'm a girl."

"Girl, nothing. You got me for two bucks."

"Can I have the two dollars in quarters so I can play video games?"

"Yeah, sure, kid. Here, give this to Reuben at the bar."

Emily happily skipped over to the bar. Some players who worked the circuit used a set list as a reminder of which songs to play at a gig. Sometimes the songs were the performer's favorites, and some were audience requests. However, a set list was made up, and it had to be a perfect one-act play. I never used a set list. I was always more comfortable feeling out the audience for what they wanted to hear.

I figured if you remembered the words and music for thirty to fifty songs, then remembering the titles would be a cinch. I remembered every song by heart. That way, I built my sets based on the general mood of the crowd or by request. I loved it when the audience requested a song, and I loved the challenge of pleasing the audience with that request. I never forgot that requests equaled tips, and tips equaled cash. It wasn't any more basic than that. The tips were especially good when a celebrity or a politician showed up. Nobody wanted to look like a tightwad in front of famous people, so I cashed in at those times.

Near the end of my third season, there was one really fabulous night that would stand out forever. The Bronx

Borough President, Herman Badillo, and renowned Latin bandleader, Tito Puente, came for dinner at the Seascape. They both stopped in the lounge for drinks and were pestered by autograph hounds, but they were gentlemen and graciously signed napkins, menus, and receipts. Once both men were served, Tommy motioned for me to play some Latino music.

I started out with an old ballad entitled "Perfidia." Mr. Badillo really loved it, and he raised his glass to me. The people just hammered me with applause. I was so proud. Tito Puente then asked me to play "Me and Julio Down by the Schoolyard." It was strange that this musical giant wanted to hear a pop song, but I wasn't about to refuse a man of his celebrity. So, I gave it my best Latin rhythm on the guitar, and the people started clapping. The smile on Tito Puente's face was a mile wide when the chorus came out. Both gentlemen went to dinner, but not before they shook my hand and thanked me for playing especially for them. I felt like a superstar. What a privilege it was to perform for them. The party they were with and the men themselves filled my brandy snifter with tips. I almost didn't want to accept them, but at the end of the night, I counted up over two hundred bucks in tips. The money was great, but the music made me feel alive.

It was the Fourth of July weekend, and the restaurant was slow that night. Every other weekend, the place was jumping from eight p.m. till midnight. Sometimes people just needed to get away from the city and from. I'd gone on short stay vacations during the week, making sure I was back by Friday to play the gig. It would have been nice to get a fill-in musician to cover my gig for the weekend. I could've gotten away for a few days, but the fill-in would probably have weaseled their way into my gig, and I would've lost it. Musicians were cutthroat with each other's gigs if the price was right, and even though this gig got old at times, it still gave me a pretty penny for a night's work.

A few weeks into July, a man and woman walked in, and the woman was swearing at him up one side and down the other. Damn it, if she wasn't laying a ration of shit on him, the likes of which I'd never heard before. The poor guy just stood there and took it. He must have felt like a shit sandwich. I remember having more than a few heated arguments with Ellen. She had that fiery Irish temper, complete with throwing inanimate objects when she wanted to express her deepest disdain for me. I'd had sergeants in the Army holler right in my face, but that lady gave out verbal abuse to the Nth power. Nobody should have to put up with that. She belittled the man beyond description and called him names I'd never heard. I wanted to say something, but I kept my mouth shut. I finally listened to that little voice that said, "Mind your own damn business." The couple's table was ready as their name was announced: "Miller, party of two." I was thankful for the quiet that ensued.

I continued to play through the remainder of the evening. The couple came back into the lounge after dinner. They sat down quietly, and I thought, "Oh my God, this is scary." The couple hadn't said a word since they came back into the lounge. I took advantage of the quietude and started to play one of my favorite songs. It was a beautiful ballad called "I'm Easy." It was written by Keith Carradine back in 1976 and used in a movie called "Nashville." It had some of the best music and lyric combinations I'd ever heard. I got to the third verse, and the words took on a life of their own with a breathy timbre. All of a sudden, the woman got up and took the man by the hand, and led him out the door. I didn't know what to think. Was she going to start slamming him again, or was it over for the night, or was it over, period? It was anybody's guess. About three weeks later, the woman and her guy showed up at the restaurant as I was setting up for the evening. She came over to me, and I was a little unsettled when she started to speak.

"Excuse me."

"Yes, can I help you?"

"No, but I owe you an apology."

"For what?" I asked.

"I don't know if you remember this, but a few weeks ago, my husband and I came here for dinner. We had an argument before arriving, and I really took out my anger on him pretty bad."

"I remember, but I try not to eavesdrop on anyone's conversation."

"Well, you didn't have to eavesdrop because I really tore into him that night. I embarrassed my husband and myself, and I'm really sorry you had to hear it. When we came out from dinner, you played one of our favorite songs—'I'm Easy'."

"Yeah, it's one of my favorites too. I think you got up and left after the song was over."

"Yes, I did. I took my husband by the hand. We got in the car and went home without a word said. I took him upstairs to the bedroom and made love to him.

I cried and told him how sorry I was to have belittled him like that in public. I begged him to please forgive me. My husband, the loving gentleman that he is, just smiled, and we went to sleep. I had to come back here to apologize to you as well. I owe that to you and him."

"No need to apologize to me, ma'am, but is everything okay now?"

"Yes, it is. Thank you. I just wanted you to know that it was the song you sang that reminded me of why I love my husband, and I thank you for it."

"You're most welcome, ma'am."

I know that music is a powerful communicator, but I never thought anything I played would instill passion or heal a wound. I guess music transcends the bounds of rational explanation.

In May 1985, I marched with twenty-five thousand of my veteran brothers and sisters across the Brooklyn Bridge down to the new Vietnam Veterans Memorial on Water Street. We poured into town like a band of gypsies in faded olive drab and blue jeans, but we didn't care. This was our day. Through the streets and down the Canyon of Heroes, we walked shoulder to shoulder, getting in the faces of those same news people who called us "baby killers" back in the sixties and seventies. When Bruce Springsteen released the song "Born in the USA," he gave the veterans a voice. We couldn't be ignored anymore, not by the military, the VA, the media, or anybody. We were together, we had survived, and we were almost home.

Well, the end of an era had finally come. It was November and the close of my fifth season at the Seascape. Emily hadn't come to see me perform much during that last season. She was busy hanging out with her friends, who talked about everything—including boys. Emily turned eleven in December, just about the time when Tommy called and asked me to perform at the Christmas party. I said yes, but I told him that this would be my last gig. He just laughed.

"What? You gotta be kiddin' me. Why ya wanna stop for? You can't stop."

"Ya havin' too much fun down here, and da' crowd loves ya."

"I know, Tommy, and I really appreciate you giving me a break and all, letting me play there over the years, but I have to move on and find my own music. I'm tired of playing everybody else's songs all the time. I have to find out if I have any songs in me. And I think I'd like to do dinner like everybody else instead of working and watching them at dinner. It's getting old."

"I can't blame ya, kid, but whaddya expect ta find?"

"I don't know, Tommy. Maybe there's nothing out there past what I can see, but I have to go take a look."

"Well, you take care, kid. Ya welcome back anytime."

"Thanks, Tommy. You've been great to me."

"Yeah, dats becuz I'm a great guy, ya know?"

"Yeah, I know, Tommy—and so does everybody else."

"Yeah, dats right!"

What a character. I came to miss that guy and his wise guy Bronx accent. I even missed the Seascape Restaurant that I must've passed a dozen or more times, but Yonkers and its familiar streets were where I lived and grew up, but it was far from being home.

This chapter contains dialogues between two Newfoundland dogs.

The dialogue is noted between three bullets.

Chapter 9: The Bear Dog

After leaving the Seascape Restaurant, I began spending a lot more time at Thwaite's Marina. Jack Scully ran the excursion service to the smaller islands in the sound. Jack was an old friend from childhood, and he approached me at the restaurant about giving him a hand running the marina on my days off from driving the limousine. The job was basically to make sure the boats were safe enough to take on passengers and to keep the crew clean and sober. Island men tended to drink more than they should.

Being brought up on the island, boating was second nature to me, and I had no problem getting the crew to toe the line. Jack paid me well enough, but I still drove the limousine regularly to maintain a decent bank account. As Emily got older, she needed new clothes and school stuff, and I had to make sure there was enough money. I didn't want to relive the old days when I had to scratch for pennies. Combined with playing an occasional gig for the local fire department and money left over from my VA school benefits, I did all right financially. I managed to take a course each semester at Iona College. Another three semesters, and I could graduate.

There were two "dock dogs" that hung out around the marina: Byron and Abbey. They were big dogs—real big! Abbey was a Newfoundland, sometimes called a "Newf" or "Newfie." Byron was part Newfoundland and part German shepherd, but he was equally massive. They were friendly enough and really no bother. Legend has it that Newfoundland dogs were descendants of the Norse Bear Dog. They had to weigh at least ninety pounds each, but they were pure love and wouldn't hurt a fly. The children loved them. When Emily came to visit, she and the dogs were inseparable, but then so were Abbey and Byron. The three of them were pretty much a team. I loved it when Emily came to visit. She was so happy to be around the dogs, the passengers, and the dock people. I felt as responsible for the dogs as I did for Emily, so I made sure they got enough to eat and had a place of their own. Home to them was the boat shed at the marina. They slept in a rowboat that was converted into a bed by some kid who worked there one summer. He took a liking to the dogs and fixed up a corner of the boat shed where they could move about easily. I fed them, but so did everyone else. They pretty much belonged to everybody and nobody. Depending on how you looked at it, life could have been worse. The dogs had each other for protection and companionship. Their only concern was survival—where to sleep, get food and stay dry. The biggest worry I had was that sometimes the dogs wandered off to the tall grass near the trees, which was right next to the New York City Police Department Firing Range. They went there when they wanted to sleep or cool down in the summer. It worried me a bit, but at least they were together. Dogs fight with each other over food and turf, much like people do, but not for the same reason. Most dogs only attack if they are rabid or to protect their pups. Newfies never attack, nor do they defend themselves even when provoked. They just run away or protect themselves by using their massive bodies as a shield.

Newfoundland dogs are the gentlest of creatures, and stories of them saving humans from drowning are countless. The coat of the Newfoundland has two layers of fur—one for warmth and one to repel water. They have weblike feet for paddling and a tail like a rudder. You could almost call them a boat with fur. They have low jowls on their mouth called flues that act as extra skin to grip the hand of a human in their mouth without hurting it during a rescue. They have sweetness in their face, especially their eyes. The only way to describe them is to say they have "I love you" eyes. There is a childlike innocence about them, almost like they are humans in a dog's body. They like being around people, and they really don't like being alone. They are especially good with children. They absolutely love the snow and the water—and they love to play. Having them at the marina helped me get through the times when I missed Emily.

I read once that Lord Byron, the eighteenth-century poet, wrote the following poem after the death of his own Newfoundland dog:

"Near this spot are deposited the remains of one who possessed beauty without vanity, strength without insolence, courage without ferocity, and all the virtues of man without his vices."

We could learn a lot from Newfies. Unfortunately, people are the only life form who hurt each other for sport or greed— or just for the hell of it. Mean people are their biggest enemy. Many dogs get kicked and beaten for no reason, but it came as a surprise to the locals when I gave them a taste of their own medicine. They thought it was funny to throw firecrackers at the dogs. The incident usually ended when someone called the police after the situation came to blows. I had no problem tossing a beating to anyone who beat a dog.

***

" It feels like summer is going to be early, Abbey."

"Yes, it does feel that way."

"Do you think it'll be bad like the last one?"

"I can only guess. I hope Ray comes soon with the food."

"He's probably having food after being in that house with all the noise and lights."

"Yes. Many odd lights and strange sounds come from there. Sometimes the others come out of the house and fall down, and then they laugh about it. Strange ones, the others."

"I've seen Ray fall down too, but he doesn't laugh, though. Most times, his eyes are filled with water. He doesn't seem happy."

"I agree, Byron. I just wish he didn't go to that house with all the noise and lights so much, and he should stay away from the water. One of these times, he might fall into the water and not dry. He just shouldn't be near the water."

"Oh, Abbey, you're being foolish. Ray can take care of things."

"Yes, but he has no one. We have us, but he is alone."

"Well, he has Emily, and he has us for friends, so he's not really alone."

"I guess so, but I'm sad for him. The only time he seems happy is when he sings or when Emily comes to visit. She's such a lovely child."

"Yes, and she gives us that nice mackerel when she comes. She's a good child. And speaking of mackerel, we should have the food soon. It's morning time, and I need the food right about now, Abbey."

"You seem to need the food more than just at morning time, Byron."

"I like the food time, and so do you. It's a good thing Ray comes by in the morning. I just wish he had come early before his sleep time. He will probably pour the food from the large sack. I won't call it tasty like the mackerel, but I guess it's good for us, eh, Abbey?"

"I'm glad for whatever he brings us and what the Bear Dog allows."

"So am I, but wouldn't you like some nice salmon?"

"Oh, Byron, just be thankful for what Ray and the others give us for food. Look, here comes Ray. He has two small sacks with him."

"Maybe we'll get salmon, eh Abbey?"

"Hmm—maybe we will, Byron."

***

I knew the dogs were ready for chow. I had mackerel and Eukanuba for them. Byron and Abbey weren't picky eaters, but they loved it when I brought salmon or mackerel. It was their equivalent of chocolate. Their water bowls were two four-quart pans from the diner. I filled them from a hose on the side of the boat shed. While I tried to fill up their water bowls, they tried to drink from the hose. I hadn't a clue as to why, but they loved drinking from the hose. Maybe it was the gushing wetness or the fact that it seemed to be an endless supply of water. They just couldn't seem to get enough, and they always got totally drenched. It was so funny to see them all wet as they shook off the excess water, but after all, was said and done, they were just being Newfies. They were water dogs, and the wetter they got, the happier they got.

Most times, the dock people fed the dogs leftovers from the diner next door or fish from Thwaites Restaurant. The fish was okay, but people's food really wasn't good for them. They preferred leftovers because they tasted better than dry dog food. The dogs pretty much gobbled their food, and once they were finished eating, they'd sleep for a while. After a nap, they usually looked for a nice clean place to do their morning constitutional, and then it was down to the water to wash and hang out. Sometimes they'd walk up and down City Island Avenue and mooch treats from anyone they could. All they had to do was walk by the bakery, and the lady inside gave them cookies.

If they stopped by the fish market, the fishmonger gave them each a mackerel. The dogs had their act down to a tee. They knew just how to pour on that Newfie charm and who to hit up for treats. They were great dogs, and I was crazy about them.

***

" I really hope Byron gets back soon. He went to watch the water for the children. They shouldn't be in the water. They could be hurt. Why do the others let them go in the water? Foolish others. Children shouldn't be in the water if they're not washing with others—I just don't know why they do that."

***

A few weeks passed, and the tourists started pouring into the island. It was about mid-season, and one of the touring boats had engine problems. I told Scully I'd take care of it because, most times, it was just a carburetor that needed cleaning or a filter that needed to be replaced. Needless to say, maintenance on a boat was never-ending. If it didn't need engine work, then preventive maintenance had to be done, or it needed painting, or this and that. I'd heard an adage that said there were two great days when you owned a boat—the day you bought it and the day you sold it. It was a bottomless pit for your bank account; however, for those who had deep pockets, it was of little concern. It was just as I'd thought. The carburetor was clogged, and the air filters needed to be replaced. Normally, this was routine maintenance, and it was done at scheduled intervals, but it had been overlooked with the early boat tours at the marina. The tours didn't usually begin until Mother's Day, when everybody wanted to take their mom out for a boat ride and act like a millionaire for 45 minutes. The season got warm early back in mid-March, which was irregular but not totally out of the norm.

It was Memorial Day weekend, the start of the peak season, and already the boats needed repairs. I went up to the boat shack to get the parts I needed, and look who was hanging out on the dock, soaking up the breeze like a pair of drunken sailors: Byron and Abbey. Man, if that's a dog's life, then I want to be a dog. If I hadn't known better, I would have sworn those dogs sucked down a few beers and grooved on too many Jimmy Buffett albums. I played with the Newfs for a bit, grabbed the parts I needed, and headed back down to the water.

***

" *I wonder where Ray went with those things, Byron.*"

"*He's going down toward the boats. I guess he's working.*"

"*I wish he would stay away from the water. Why does he have to go there?*"

"*Abbey, he's working for his friend. He'll be all right.*"

"*You sires are all the same. You never worry about anything.*"

"*You're being foolish, Abbey. He knows how to take care of things.*"

"*Yes, but he shouldn't be near the—oh dear, Byron, something must have fallen in the water. Do you know that sound like the big hooks make when the others throw it in the water when they come in from the sea? And I heard a loud voice just before the water made that sound.*"

"*I heard the same thing, Abbey, but the others are always throwing things in the water.*"

"*But this sounded like some big thing went in the water. I'm going down to look.*"

"*Oh, all right, Abbey, we'll both go. Look! Ray is in the water. He's not moving. We have to get the others.*"

"*No time, Byron. Go get the others. I'm going in the water to get Ray.*"

"*Abbey, wait!*"

97

"No time, Byron! Go get the others!"

***

Running as fast as she could, Abbey ended the spirited sprint from the dock with a long dive into the sound, giving herself enough distance to get as close to Ray as she could. She swam furiously in between buoys and boats. Meanwhile, Byron ran from the dock to the marina office and frantically barked as he tried to get the others' attention. At first, no one gave much thought to the barking dog that jumped up and down on his front legs as he desperately tried to alert someone to the danger at hand. Finally, one of the tourists took notice. Byron motioned his head toward the water, and the gentleman followed the Newf as he ran toward the boat slip where Ray had fallen.

"There's someone floating in the water," the man cried as he reached for a nearby floatation device and dashed toward the water's edge. Not one for patience, especially with someone in the water, Abbey grabbed a piece of Ray's shirt and swam as fast as she could, pulling him toward the dock, now muddled with others. By the time Abbey got to the slip, Ray's friend Scully was there. He and one of his workers pulled Ray out of the water.

"All right, everybody gets back and let him have some air," Scully shouted. He started first aid immediately as he breathed into Ray's mouth, held his nose, and pushed on his chest. It took several attempts, but Ray eventually coughed up a geyser with enough water to get it all over everyone who stood nearby.

"Okay, talk to me, Ray," Scully said. "You okay, buddy?" I motioned my head up and down slightly, and it felt like I'd be all right. The others dispersed as soon as the paramedics arrived.

"Let them through. Come on, everybody, move back," Scully ordered. The paramedics treated the bump on my head and gave me oxygen until my breathing was stabilized. I resisted a little, but Scully pretty much forced me to go with the paramedics to the hospital.

As the ambulance pulled out, Scully walked toward the two exhausted Newfoundlands. They were heroes. Byron and Abbey saved my life. Scully stooped down and pulled the dogs close. He whispered, "You guys saved Ray. No one here will ever forget that. You've earned yourselves a place today. Now, let's see if we can't find you both some salmon."

I didn't remember much during the ride home from the hospital, except I'd be dead if it weren't for those dogs. I remembered coming topside after replacing the filters and cleaning the carburetor. I must've slipped and hit my head somewhere on the deck. The next thing I remembered was coughing up a lot of water and having a bad headache. Anyway,

Scully told me that Abbey pulled me from the water to the dock while Byron ran for help. They are pretty amazing dogs, but I already knew that.

***

" *Where are you going, Byron?*"

"*I need to move my leg a little. It still hurts after that fight with Mephisto. I'm going to walk over by the tall grass where it's cool under the trees.*"

"*Should I come with you?*"

"*No, Abbey. I just want to walk and sit by myself for a while. I'll be back soon.*"

As he walked away, Abbey began to wonder what Byron was thinking.

"*Hmm, Byron never walks by himself. Things must be on his mind. I wonder if it's the coming summer. He didn't feel good during the last one. Maybe he's just tired and needs rest time. He likes the tall grass, and it's so nice and cool under the trees. We usually go there to sleep on hot days. The children don't go there ever. Maybe it's because of the short, loud sounds that we hear sometimes. I'm afraid of the sounds, but they don't seem to bother Byron. I just wish I knew what he was thinking. I worry about him. We've been together since just after we were pups. We have cared for each other since that time. He has been a good mate to me, always sharing his food. Byron protects me from the mean others who hurt dogs and from that bad Mephisto. I didn't want Byron to fight him, but he needed to be stopped. He was hurting the other dogs and taking their food—but mostly, I didn't want him to hurt me again. Hmm, there's Ray! I think I'll go walk with him. He's so good to Byron and me. I'm really glad he didn't lose all his air when he fell into the water. I wonder where the others go when they lose all their air. Maybe they go to a place like we do and be with the Bear Dog."*

***

" Hey, Abbey girl, how're you doing? Where's Byron? Is he wandering by the bakery again? That dog has the biggest sweet tooth.

Where are you going, girl? Hey, wait for me. You run faster. No, don't go near the trees. Abbey, stop! Abbey, stop! Why are you going toward the trees? Is that Byron? No wonder she's going there. What the hell? Oh my God, he's heading toward the dunes!"

The NYPD firing range was adjacent to the dunes along the northwest side of City Island. No one ever went near the range. Island children were taught as babies not to go near the dunes. There were signs clearly posted so that no accidents happened, but dogs couldn't read, so it didn't do them much good. I started yelling at the top of my voice for Byron to stop. I ran as fast as I could until I got to where I thought he could hear me.

***

" Byron, stop! Byron, Byron—stop! Byron, no! Stop! Stop! Byron!"

***

Byron must've heard me because he turned around to look. Abbey was only a few feet away from him when I heard gunshots. Byron wandered too close to the range.

Abbey flinched every time she heard a shot fired. She lay on the ground shaking, too afraid to follow Byron, but she barked at a rapid pace to get his attention. It hadn't done any good. Byron found his way onto the police department shooting range. In a New York minute, Byron was dodging police cadet bullets. A bullet didn't care what it hit—men, women, children, or animals. A bullet had no conscience. I ran onto the range like a raving lunatic, and the firing stopped. They stopped firing for a man but not for a dog. It said a lot for the species, didn't it?

The range commander ran toward me with a look that could and would kill.

"What the hell are you doing out here, you moron, trying to get yourself killed?"

"No, I was trying to get the dog off the firing range. It's a good thing that your people can't shoot worth a damn."

"They're in training to be police officers, so don't give me any of your lip, or I'll cuff you right here. Are we clear?"

"Yeah, we're clear about one thing. God help us if these guys become cops."

"Okay, wise guy. Can you do better?"

"Better than those dimwits, I'm sure."

"Well then, why don't you take your sorry civilian ass down to One Police Plaza and put in an application. Let's see if you keep your mouth from getting your ass in trouble. Now get the hell off my range."

Figuring that jail wasn't something I wanted to experience, I called the dogs to follow me, and we started back toward the marina. I kept thinking about what the range commander had said. I never considered applying to the New York City Police Department.

It never crossed my mind to become a cop, but suddenly it seemed possible, especially since I opened up my big mouth. I was nine years old, and I still didn't have a career. I couldn't drive the limousine forever, and I had to think about some kind of pension and finishing college. I also wanted to get married again someday. I decided to jump on the train the next day and put in an application. I didn't mind being wrong about things. I had lots of practice at it, but I hated it when somebody else was right.

Well, it was official. I'd been accepted for training at the New York City Police Academy. Who the hell would've guessed?! I figured my background check must've told them that I wasn't an ax murderer. I never got arrested or anything, so I guess I was within the acceptable range of suitable human beings. My mom was pleased, but I knew she'd worry, especially about me carrying a weapon. Hopefully, I'd never have to use it, but if it was them or me, then there would be no contest.

"Hey, Scully, I need a favor."

"Sure, Ray. Whatever you need."

"I'm off to the Police Academy next week, and I'd like you to look after the dogs. Can you do that for me?"

"Ray, those dogs are special, but I don't have to tell you that. They're like kids, you know? Byron and Abbey are families down here at the marina. I'll look after them and make sure they get fed."

"Thanks, Scully. I hate to sound cliché, but it looks like God does work in mysterious ways. Who would have guessed that He'd use two Newfoundland dogs for lifeguards? Far be it for me to question it. They saved my ass."

"That they did, Ray, and you saved theirs. I'll make sure they don't wander by the dunes anymore."

"Yeah, please, will you, Scully?"

"Sure thing, pal. Just make sure you say goodbye to them."

Saying goodbye to Byron and Abbey wasn't easy. Scully was right. Those dogs were like my kids. I cared about them and looked after them just like I did Emily. They were sensitive, those Newfoundlands. I couldn't stop my own tears when I went to say goodbye.

"Hey guys, listen. I have to talk to you. I won't be around every day like I usually am. I got a different job now, and I have to be in Manhattan every day. Scully's going to look after you like I did, okay? He'll take good care of you, and I want you to listen to him. You have to be careful out there every day. I'll stop by and see you when I'm not working. I love you guys so much." I held them close like they were my own children.

***

" Ray is sad, Byron. Did you see all the water in his eyes? What do you think is wrong?"

"I don't think Ray will be coming to see us like he used to do. Maybe he's working somewhere else. Ray hasn't been coming by in the morning. His friend, Scully, has been bringing us food. Maybe Ray is going somewhere. What do you think, Abbey?"

"I don't know, Byron. Maybe you're right. I just know he's sad. I think he needs a mate. He doesn't have anyone."

"Well, if he's going somewhere, Abbey, I hope he finds a mate. I will miss him. He has been a good friend to us."

"*I'll miss him and Emily too, Byron. I think we should ask the Bear Dog to keep him safe.*"

"*Yes, that is a good idea, Abbey.*"

***

I'm not much for praying, seeing as though I'm still angry with God, but I asked Him to watch over the dogs while I was away.

Chapter 10: Rookie Days

I'd often wondered how I arrived at certain situations. What I started to realize was the more I knew, the less I understood. I thought about the things I'd seen and the faces I'd been to, and I wondered why I hadn't ended up on the streets or gotten myself killed in the war. It was still a mystery to me, and I couldn't help but think that maybe it was "divine intervention," as my mother called it. Maybe there really was a God who saved me for a greater purpose. I didn't have a clue, but if there was a greater purpose, where did I fit in the grand scheme of things—if there was a grand scheme?

I got through the police academy without much trouble. It was just as I thought—a combination of boot camp and parochial school. Most of the other candidates were between twenty-one and twenty-three years old. At twenty-nine, they were all kids compared to me. A high and tight haircut, topped with some spit and polish, and I was a sharp candidate. I kept everything spotless. There were no mistakes in my appearance. I remembered an old sergeant I had in the Army who used to say, "You have to cooperate to graduate." That's what exactly I did.

I took it all seriously because I could get killed on those mean streets if I made a mistake. There was no margin for error, especially when I was on the job. I couldn't afford to lose a fight or give up ground because it would cost me my life. It was as dangerous as the rice paddies of Vietnam, and there were similarities. I had my assignment, patrolled the perimeter in the area of operation, and kept a watchful eye for anything suspicious. In Vietnam, I established a rapport with the locals and tried to keep us alive and home safe. A police officer had a similar mission: to protect and serve the public. That went for us; that went for them. Vietnam and New York City seemed to be two sides of the same coin.

My first assignment was to a Neighborhood Stabilization Unit (NSU) for six months. It was an adjustment period as I familiarized myself with the surrounding area. As a rookie, I was assigned to traffic duty and crowd control. I also learned how to safeguard evidence at a crime scene and to do some low-level PR with the locals. Most of the locals were decent, hard-working people who wanted to be left to their own business. They wanted to know they were safe. I took an oath to do the best job I could, and my word meant something, just like it always did. I wasn't going to fool myself with idealistic notions of saving New York City from the bad guys. I was there to do the 'job,' put in my time, and hope to God that I didn't get killed for something stupid. I saw enough senseless killing during the war, and I wasn't so foolish to have thought that I could change people or circumstances. I had to remind myself constantly to take what I knew and do the best I could. Sometimes I thought about the places I'd been, the things I'd done, and the close calls I had.

I could have been killed on any given day in any number of instances, both during Vietnam and after. I wondered many times why my friends were killed, and I survived. I was no better than them, so why were they dead? Better yet, why was I still alive? I thought maybe God had selection criteria for those who lived and died. How had I gotten to this place in my life? Luck? I doubted it. Nobody was that lucky.

My NSU assignment was the 41st Precinct—an area in the South Bronx commonly known as Fort Apache. It was the area along Southern Boulevard from 149th to 156th Street. It was predominately made up of Latino and Black working-class people, most of whom were decent people. There was a bodega about every seven hundred feet that sold everything from fried chicken to Pampers. The people there knew me, and I believed they trusted me. That God-forsaken place was a far cry from the safe, serene neighborhood where I grew up. There were no gutted, burned-out buildings, back-alley drug deals, or streetwalkers on City Island Avenue. We had seafood restaurants, yachts, and tourists with money. The streets of City Island weren't paved with gold, but they weren't littered with crack vials either; however, there in that desolate South Bronx area of poverty and despair, no one—not even the wrongdoer—could survive without fear. They were not afraid of jail, or else they wouldn't risk the crime, and they surely weren't afraid of decent people, but they were afraid of each other. To live fast and die young was the best they could expect. What I gathered from my brothers and sisters in blue was that I must have pissed somebody off in a previous life to get that assignment. There were lots of bad guys in that neighborhood, and they were not all guys. They came in all shapes and sizes, from seven to seventy years old, and everything in between. We had cocaine dealers, seven-year-olds running numbers, teenage gangs, teenage prostitutes, welfare fraud, illegal immigrants, and too many guns. We were there to protect and serve the public—the good, hard-working public who helped pay our salary—and I learned from the get-go that members of the criminal element were also public. It was against regulations to use corporal punishment on criminals, but it was done from time to time when a perp tried to play innocent. There were no innocent perps on those streets. All of them were out hustling for whatever they could get away with.

I didn't try to impress anybody there. I just listened and watched. I was told to pay particular attention to the gangs in my sector. The Savage Skulls hung out in their dilapidated clubhouse on the corner of 152nd and Kelly Streets, but they weren't alone. The Ghetto Brothers and the Latin Kings also laid claim to the area. Those were the gangs that terrorized everyone and anyone in a ten-block radius with threats and violence against young and old alike. They took what little money those people had, and the decent people lived in fear. There could have been a building ablaze or somebody bleeding and lying in the gutter, and we would never have known unless we saw it go down. Too many crimes were never reported to the police because the people were so terrified of the gangs. Without a complaint, we couldn't do anything. Sometimes those we protected and served didn't realize how powerless we were without their help.

After six months in the NSU, I was assigned to the 44th Precinct. The area of operation was from the East River to Webster Avenue, running east and west, and 149th Street to Mount Eden Avenue, running north and south. At first, I was on foot patrol. Eventually, I was assigned to a sector and a partner. I showed up an hour early every day, suited up and on time for roll call. The sergeant gave pertinent information about goings on in the sector—things like known perps, gangs acting up, and the citywide color of the day.

After roll call, I checked the radio car with my new partner and rolled out into another working night in the badlands— one more battle in the urban war. We were out there to do the job, but the primary goal was to come back alive after our tour, so we could go out and do it all again the next day. The procedure was always the same: We opened up the locker, suited up, and holstered the cold, hard-tempered steel that could be the difference between life and death. In many ways, being on the job was like being in Vietnam; only the uniform was blue. Like Vietnam, I knew my brothers would come for me if the unforgiving streets tried to take me down.

I was paired up with another patrolman named Zack Tillman. He seemed like a decent enough guy, and I felt like I could count on him to cover my back, but for some reason, it didn't appear that his heart was in the job anymore. After riding together for a few months, we warmed up to each other and started sharing a little about our personal lives. Like me, he was born and bred in the Bronx. A real Yankees fan, he grew up in the Inwood section of the Northwest Bronx. Zack was divorced, but he didn't have any kids, and it didn't bother him one bit with all the women he had in his hip pocket. Zack talked a lot about women. He had what we guys called an "eternal hard-on." He also talked about moving on to bigger and better things, like starting his own business, you know, being your own boss and stuff. It all sounded like a bullshit get-rich-quick scheme to me, but maybe he felt that way because he'd been on the job for five years. In five years, maybe I'd feel the same way.

One day, Zach asked, "So, Ray, how long have you been on the job now?"

"It'll be a year soon."

"What do you think of the job—I mean, really?"

"I'm fine with it. I chose it."

"You really like being a cop?"

"Yeah, Zack, I really like being a cop."

"You don't think of doing something else for a living?"

"Well, I wanted Neil Young's job when he left Crosby, Stills, and Nash, but I guess they never got my letter, so I decided to join the force. Don't you like being on the job anymore, Zack?"

"Sure, but you gotta think ahead. Look at all the bookies and dealers. Hell, they got tons of money stashed away while we work every day in this sewer. Sometimes I feel like a garbage man, always picking up trash, day in and day out. The only thing is that the trash we pick up has more money than we'll ever see. And what do we get for our trouble? A fifty percent pension if we live to make twenty years."

"I don't know about that, Zack. I mean, what about everybody else? Yeah, we have to get the trash off the street, but what about the good people? We're all they have for protection."

"God, you're such a boy scout, Ray."

"Maybe so, but we all need protection sometimes."

"Yeah, well, I'm not looking for anybody to protect me. I'm just looking after myself. C'mon, let's go grab a coffee."

"Sure, boss," I said smilingly.

I thought about what Zack had said for the rest of my tour. He had a point. The criminals would always have more than we did. I had more pride in how I made a living, and I wasn't looking over my shoulder to see who was trying to get me. Still, I couldn't begrudge him for the way he felt.

Day after day, over the next few years, I lived in a series of foot pursuits, open and closed cases, rousted troublemakers, and digested radio codes that oozed out over the air. Most of them were vehicle accidents or family disputes that required more social work than police work. Basically, what you tried to do was keep husbands and wives from beating the hell out of each other and their kids. Living in a South Bronx tenement in ninety-degree weather on the sixth floor with no air conditioning would drive anyone to violence. What we really had was a keg of gunpowder that begged for a lighted match.

Vehicle accidents weren't pretty either, especially when somebody got hurt. DWI joyriders and car thieves were the common offenders, but I'd seen just as many well-dressed Mercedes-Benz and BMW owners who had their fair share of fender benders too. Vehicle fatalities were pretty gruesome, and after seeing enough of them, you grew a thick skin because you knew it was going to happen again, but I never got used to seeing a dead child. In Vietnam, it turned my stomach to see the body parts of children splattered all over a rice paddy. It was no different here, only the location had changed. Local kids got killed in car accidents, ran with gangs, robbed stores, played with guns, and sometimes were killed at the hands of a relative. At those times, with my stomach in a knot, I just looked up and asked, "Why?"

The 44th Precinct was littered with its share of drug dealers. Like pestilence, they were everywhere. The way I figured it, dealers were the result of an over-consuming society with an insatiable appetite for instant gratification and self-indulgence. Drugs were no longer just used by the lowlifes aptly illustrated in newspapers and movies. The drug trade had found its way to some of the most exclusive addresses on Park Avenue.

During every tour of duty, there was a deal going down on almost every street. Most times, the wheelers and dealers were gone before I could say 'freeze,' but every once in a while, I saw a deal in progress. I knew I'd seen the dealer before somewhere down the line. I'd eyeball him, he'd see me, and the dealer would take off like a bat out of hell with his ass on fire. Sometimes I said to myself, "Oh no, he's not getting away this time." I hit the lights, siren, and gas. The next thing I knew, I was hauling ass up a one-way street, and I saw the scum drop the stash in a dumpster. At the end of the one-way street, there'd be an alley where the car couldn't go, so I came to a screeching halt and went after him on foot. Now I was really pissed. He was digging it out toward a chain link fence. He was younger and faster, and he had better footwear than I did. If I could, I'd have given him a summons for having illegal sneakers. Now the punk was almost at the fence. He got cocky and desperate. He made a flying leap from five feet away, thinking he could grab hold of the fence halfway up. But his fingers didn't make it. He slipped and fell flat on his face.

I grabbed him by the seat of his pants and flung him against the wall to knock the wind out of his sails. Then he was on his face with my knee in his back. I cuffed him, hoisted him to his feet, and gave him an industrial-strength attitude adjustment.

I busted my hump on those streets for six years, and it finally paid off when I was chosen for detective duty. Detectives were selected in a pretty clear-cut manner. The criteria were a job well done, good police work in the field, a good arrest and investigation record, and a good attitude. It took about five years before a police officer was even considered a detective. The officer was usually someone who used his head and thought on his feet. The brass looked closely at the officer's arrest record for details, like arrests without injury to other officers or civilians—that even included perps. I focused on busting every drug dealer I could, probably because my brother got involved with them for a while, and it messed him up for a good long time. I did a decent job out there, and I guess the right people took notice.

I was assigned a new partner named Mike D'Ambrosio. My former partner, Zack Tillman, didn't seem to mind one way or the other. I guess he really had plans of his own, but it bothered me a little that he didn't wish me well or anything. Mike was an eighteen-year veteran cop with eleven years as a detective. He was well-liked by his fellow detectives, and he was flat-out known as a good cop. The brass especially liked him. From what I heard on day one, the other detectives teased him a bit and called him 'preacher' because he was a practicing Christian who tried to live according to Scripture. He even carried a King James Bible with him in the radio car. Mike was always trying to lead people to God, and he was known to quote from Scripture to his brother officers. Knowing cops the way I did, they probably didn't agree with his 'preaching,' but it was obvious they respected him.

I remember the day he came into the squad room to introduce himself.

"Hi—Mike D'Ambrosio."

"Ray MacDonald. Good to meet you."

"Same here, Ray. Where are you from?"

"Yonkers. What about you?"

"Oh, I'm a Yonkers boy myself, born and raised. Were you in the service?"

"I was in the Army. I did a tour in Vietnam as a combat medic."

"Wow, that must've been rough. I was in the Navy on a carrier in the South Pacific—never went on shore, but we took on a lot of wounded, though."

"Yeah, a lot of that was going around then."

"Are you married, Ray?"

"I used to be. I have a teenage daughter, and she is my shining pride."

"Boy, that's great."

"What about you, Mike?"

"I'm married to my high school sweetheart. Katie is the best. We have two kids, a boy and a girl. We pretty much do things as a family—you know, like picnics, vacations, and church. Are you a church-going man, Ray?"

"No, but I hear you are."

"Is that going to bother you, Ray, because I keep a Bible in the radio car?"

"Nah, not at all. Just don't try to convert me."

"You don't need to be converted, Ray. No one does. You just have to find your way to God's path, that's all."

"If you say so, Mike."

"All right, Ray, let's go check out the car and take her for a spin. We'll grab some coffee, and I'll show you the area, and as we say in the Navy, you'll get your sea legs."

"Let's do it, Mike. I'm ready."

I had to say that I liked Mike right off the bat. He was the kind of guy who people took to immediately, like a favorite uncle. He was different from Zack and more focused, and that was good because I needed to learn from a partner whose feet were firmly planted in the job. We rode the streets every day for the next two years and worked every type of case that came our way. Usually, detectives worked in a specific area, like robbery, homicide, arson, or vice squad. We were a small division, so we pretty much did everything.

One day Mike introduced me to Christine, the administrative assistant in our police division. I couldn't take my eyes off her. Christine was so pretty. I was really taken by her. We made small talk now and then and kept anything that could be misconstrued as personal as far from the precinct as possible. Fraternizing was discouraged in the detective division, but eventually, we got to know each other and saw each other socially. It started on Christmas Eve. Emily generally spent that evening with her mother, who by that time had remarried. I usually picked her up on Christmas day, so with nothing to do, I hung out at the station after Mike went home and rechecked my write-ups. As she left, Christine asked why I was still working. I explained the situation. She suggested that we go for coffee, and then she'd go to her parents' house afterward for Christmas Eve dinner. I wasn't about to pass up an offer to spend time with her, so I dumped the idea of working that evening and opted for more pleasant company.

I finally got my degree in Criminal Justice, and Emily graduated from high school that same year. The last time I looked, she was eight years old and playing video games. She blossomed into a beautiful young woman and smart too. The following fall, she went off to college in Pennsylvania. She even managed to get a few scholarships for herself. We saw each other pretty often, but we mostly just talked on the phone. She'd grown up and was out living her young life—and that's the way it should be. We managed to get together when our schedules didn't collide, and I enjoyed the closeness with her that my father and I never had. Looking back on it, maybe it was a generational thing that distanced me from my father, but I was determined to build a good relationship with Emily, and fortunately, I succeeded.

Christmas with Emily after she graduated, was just like always—expensive but fun. I loved to watch the look on her face when she opened her presents. Unfortunately, the magic of the holiday season hadn't spilled into the New Year. Mike and I were called into the lieutenant's office. We were assigned to investigate the report of a shooting at Crotona Park. The report said that an Asian boy was shot and killed by a stray bullet, possibly during a drug deal that went south. The lieutenant told us to work the case by the book and to handle it with kid gloves. The brass didn't want anyone to have the slightest whiff that the shooting might have been racially motivated. Hearing that a child was killed shook me to the core, and I wanted the killer really bad.

We arrived at the crime scene shortly after the report had come in. The paramedics had just lifted the boy from the gutter onto the gurney. I looked at the dead boy as his family sobbed and desperately held onto each other. It infuriated me as I watched the child's blood run into a sewer. The scene was all too familiar. I remember seeing innocent blood shed in Vietnam after the Viet Cong came through a village. The memory still haunted me. At first, I wanted the perp for killing a child. Now, I wanted to empty a clip into his chest, even though the rulebook says never to get personally involved with a case.

A policeman had to think straight and focus. If he worked a case with his emotions tied up in a square knot, it would only compromise the investigation. But how could I not get emotional when a nine-year-old was lying in the street with a bullet hole in his chest? I had to tread carefully on that case and follow Mike's lead closely. He had the mileage. I was just along for the ride. I talked with the curious onlookers and hoped to get tidbits of information, but as I suspected, no one saw anything. Mike checked out the area within a fifty-meter radius as the uniformed cops talked to everybody. If you got enough information, eventually, you'd piece it together, and then the puzzle became a snapshot of the incident. The only problem was that the pieces were so damn small, which meant that sometimes you had to squat.

"Ray, take a look at this—a spent .38 caliber shell—recently fired."

"Yeah, you can still smell the powder."

"Let's take a look around and get the uniformed cops looking too. I got a feeling there's more than one of these shells lying around here somewhere."

Mike was onto something, but he wasn't saying anything I could work with. I'd just love to know what he was thinking. Me, I thought a spent .38 caliber shell meant that a cop was involved. I just didn't know to what extent. A few minutes later, one of the uniformed cops found a second spent .38 caliber shell and handed it to Mike.

"I knew it. Where'd you find it, son?"

"Over near the bench, detective."

"Good work. What's your name, patrolman?"

"Lombardi, Robert Lombardi, shield number—"

"I got it, son. Good job. See if you can help sort out some of the statements from the locals and then get back to me. My name is D'Ambrosio."

"Sure thing, detective."

"You know that rookie, Mike?"

"Nah, he's just a kid trying to do a good job. He's hungry— remind you of anybody, Ray?"

"Yeah, me about a million years ago," I said laughingly.

"What'd you find, Ray?"

"I talked with one middle-aged lady who said she took her dog out to go potty when she heard two or three loud pops, but she didn't remember seeing anything. She's gone now, but I have her information. I think she heard a lot more than she says, and she probably saw something too, but I can tell she's scared."

"Yeah, Ray, they all are. All right, let's gather up everything and head back to the house. We'll sort it out there."

Mike's composure was as level as usual. My gut told me that he knew something, but he wasn't quite ready to say anything.

"Mike, what's bothering you?"

"Something stinks about this case, Ray."

"Like what?"

"There's something about those .38 shells. I mean, magnums and assault rifles are the toys of choice for these punks out here. If you're trying to kill somebody, you'd use the gun with the biggest bang, not a pea shooter. I mean, who brings a knife to a gunfight?"

Mike was right about the weapons of choice. Unfortunately, it was usually some innocent bystander who got hurt. A child was killed, and that had gotten to both of us. I came to this job not idealistic but believing that people were basically good. Now I didn't know what to believe, and it seemed that my heart just got harder and harder with every tour of duty.

When we got back to the station, I saw some guy sitting and talking to Christine. Mike knew him. He was a Yonkers cop.

"How're you doing, Mike?"

"Oh, pretty good, Joey, and yourself?"

"I'm doing good."

"Be back in a minute. I need to use the toilet."

"So, you're MacDonald, right?"

"Yeah, that's right."

"I'm Joey Vallone, Yonkers PD."

"Yeah and—?"

"I heard you guys got a case that may involve somebody I've been trying to collar."

"Okay, so let's open up the notebooks."

"Well, I'm keeping this pretty tight, so why don't you tell me what you have, and if it matches up, we'll go from there."

"I don't know what you guys do up in Yonkers, but we don't play it that way here. Do you want to pump me for information without giving up what you know? Fat chance, Vallone. I'm not going to let you just snatch up our collar. What kind of bullshit are you trying to pull?"

"You got it all wrong, MacDonald."

"The hell I do."

I got up in his face to let him know I wasn't playing.

"Take your shit and get the hell out of here. Go back to Yonkers."

"You got some pair, MacDonald. I'm trying to catch the perps just like you."

"Well, you're not like me, so take a hike."

Joey Vallone left with a smirk on his face and a wink at Christine.

"So, did I walk in on something?"

"No, Ray, you didn't walk in on anything except me talking to family,"

Christine said smilingly.

"Family?"

"Uh-huh, first cousin."

I felt like an ass. "Sorry, Chris."

She laughed. "It's Okay, Ray. It's kind of cute to see you a little jealous."

I smiled. "Thanks."

"Ray, sometimes you guys, with your tempers, worry me a little. Can't you guys play nice?"

"Only in the sandbox, sweetie. Are we still on for dinner?"

"Yes, of course, we are," she said just as Mike came back from the men's room.

"Hey, where's Joey?"

"He went back to Yonkers—where he belongs."

"Did you guys have a—aw, Ray, what happened?"

"Nothing. He tried to pump me for info, and I sent his ass back to

Yonkers. What balls this guy has. How do you know him, Mike?"

"I worked a case with him about seven years ago. He's a good cop with a little too much attitude, just like you, but he's a decent guy."

"You have got to be kidding me. Him?"

"Yes, him. He's a cop too, and you should treat him like a brother because he's one of us."

"I don't think so, Mike. I don't trust him."

"Well, you better trust your brothers. And remember what Jesus said, "*Whatsoever you do to the least of my brothers that you do unto me.*" That's from the book of Matthew in the New Testament. You might read the Bible once in a while. It wouldn't kill you."

"Oka, Mike, I got the point."

"I hope so, Ray—Joey could be a help to us."

"Hmm, I'll take your word for it, Mike."

"Good. See you two at the restaurant later, right?"

"Yes, Mike," we said in unison.

I didn't trust Vallone, cop or not, but I trusted Mike. He never lied to me, and I could count how many times he'd been wrong on one hand. He was only thirteen years my senior, yet he felt like a father figure.

Chapter 11: Shielded

I couldn't believe I actually agreed to it, but I decided to have dinner in Yonkers with four other detectives and their wives. Seafood was everyone's first choice, but having grown up there, it would've been my last choice. I could still smell the salty air from Long Island Sound, cluttered with yachts from Great Neck to Greenwich and parts between. I tried hard to bow out of the dinner, but my brother's officers finally won me over, so I made reservations for eight at none other than the Seascape Restaurant. I figured that since we were going there, I would say hello to some old friends.

I picked up Christine at six o'clock and headed toward the Island. We talked casually about having dinner with coworkers, how good the food was, and what it was like growing up in a touristy town. Christine was a sweet girl from Pelham Bay. She was very pretty and always nicely dressed. Hers was a close-knit Italian family who were just about the nicest people you'd ever want to meet. They seemed to approve of the relationship, even though I was divorced with a small child, and they were practicing Roman Catholics. Her parents were not my biggest concern—the brass was since dating someone in your own precinct was frowned upon. My lieutenant cautioned me about seeing Christine socially since we both worked in the same precinct and people talked. I thought he was more worried about what would happen if it didn't work out since I hadn't been in a successful relationship since Lanh. Christine and I exercised enough discretion that kept the brass out of my face and off her back.

We got to the restaurant, and everyone else was already there. The cocktail lounge had changed so much since the time I performed there. Instead of live entertainment, a video jukebox stood in the place where I once played for hours. A flood of memories came over me as I nursed a bottle of Corona. I remembered especially the night that Herman Badillo and Tito Puente came in for dinner and requested songs from me. God, that was so great. Then there were the not-so-great times, like the fights in the parking lot and the woman in the lounge who had made her husband feel like two cents. But by and large, the times were good. Now and again, I could still hear the audience in my head. I missed the sound, but that was a whole lifetime ago. I asked the maître d' if Tommy was on duty. He said Tommy passed away a few years ago. I hadn't recognized the bartender or the wait staff. The owners weren't there, so I let the memory remain just that.

One thing that hadn't changed was the food. They still gave you a lot of food for your money. We all got stuffed to the gills on lobster, crab, filet of sole, and pasta. The night was great as

I hung out with my partner Mike and his wife Katie, Tommy Lucas, Billy Hohenwarter, and their wives. When I was around those guys, it was like having a family with me all the time. Nothing could take the place of blood on blood when you shared memories, and the gene pool too, but those guys were like my combat buddies from Vietnam…as close as blood. I had a great time until some so-and-so walked through the door, and it was in the form of my nemesis from the Yonkers Police Department, Joey Vallone.

"Christine," I said, "Did he know we were coming here?"

"He called and asked me what I was doing tonight, Ray. How did I know he'd show up?"

"Why did you have to tell him anything? What we do is none of his business."

"Ray, he's family," she said as Joey approached the table.

"Mike, Tommy, Billy—how you guys doing?"

"Pretty good, Joey," Mike said. "How about you?"

"I'm doing good."

"How are you doing, MacDonald?"

"It's kind of obvious, isn't it?"

"Hey, look, I'm just stopping by to say hello."

"Okay, you said it, so if you don't mind, we came out to enjoy the evening. Now you can move on."

"No need to be nasty, MacDonald. I just wanted to stop by and see my cousin. It just so happens she's with you."

"Yeah, and that's the part you want to remember."

"All right, Ray, take it easy," Mike said. "He's just making conversation."

"No, he's not, Mike. He came to break my balls because I'm here with

Christine."

Softly, she pleaded with me, "Please, Ray. Don't get into it with him."

"You know, MacDonald, one of these days, your mouth is going to get your ass into trouble."

"Yeah, well, anytime you feel 'froggy,' Vallone, go ahead and leap."

"All right, that's enough from both of you," Mike said.

"Joey, let's get a fresh drink at the bar, eh?"

"Sure, Mike, the hot air is starting to rise in here. See ya, cuz."

Christine nodded to him. I wasn't the only one who was pissed.

We realized that Joey left the restaurant when Mike came back to the table alone. He had a heart-to-heart with Joey about me, and then he pulled me aside. I knew it was my turn for the Gospel, according to Mike D'Ambrosio.

"Ray, I want you to hear me on this. I talked to Joey, and I set him straight. Now I'm going to set you straight. There's a case you're both working on, but you're getting nowhere because you both want the collar."

"What you seem to forget is that there's a family out there that needs justice and closure. They lost a child, and that's as bad as it gets. And don't you forget for a minute that I'm working on this case too? You and Joey have good intentions, but you're both too full of pride. You call yourselves police officers, but you can't just say it. You have to do it. Even the Bible says, "Be doers of the word, and not hearers only." It wouldn't hurt you to read the Scriptures or go to church once in a while. Are you hearing me, Ray?"

"I hear you, Mike."

"Okay, then let this burn in real good. You, me, and Joey are meeting up on Monday, and we will all start sharing notebooks. Got it?"

"Got it, Mike."

"He's not a bad guy, Ray, and you two are more alike than either of you want to admit."

"You want to explain that one to me, Mike?"

"He served in Vietnam with the 101st Airborne Division, so now you both got something in common. Make the call, set up the meeting, and the three of us will put our heads together. Kapish?"

"Sure, Mike. I kapish."

Mike and I sat back down at the table, and we continued with our evening. I listened when Mike talked. He hadn't been wrong in the ten years I'd known him, and I wouldn't second-guess him now. He got a little 'preachy' at times, but he was my partner. He meant well, and he'd been on the job twenty-four years, and that counted for something. Mike and his wife, Katie, were both very active in their church, and you had to respect someone who reads the Bible and tries to live by the Word of God. I listened to Mike when he talked about the Scriptures, but I couldn't say I agreed with everything he said. I just hadn't "found my way to God's path," as Mike put it.

Around nine p.m., Mike and Katie invited us all to their house for coffee. Katie made great coffee in that old Pyrex pot she had, so no one passed up the invite. They were such great people, and they had a good marriage, the kind you envied and hoped to have someday—at least I did. I would've given anything to have a marriage like that. We got to the house, and Katie put on some coffee, and then the stories started.

Sometime around midnight, Billy Hohenwarter decided that he felt like having pasta.

In total disbelief, Tommy Lucas asked, "Billy, where the hell did you put your dinner in the garage? How can you possibly be hungry?"

"I don't know, I just feel like having pasta—you know, with the garlic and oil."

"Billy, you got to be kidding me. Nobody can be that hungry right after dinner—and dessert."

Always the great hostess, Katie said, "I'll make it for you, Bill. It's no trouble."

"Nah, Katie. Don't make it on my account."

"Nonsense, Billy. We'll all have some. Who wants pasta?"

All of a sudden, three pair of hands went up. Fifteen minutes later, there we were, eating pasta with olive oil and garlic at 1 a.m. We must've been out of our minds, or else we talked ourselves hungry. It didn't matter, though. It was great just to be with those people—friends, good friends. The last time I had friends like that, I was dodging bullets in Vietnam. Now most of them were either dead or lost in America somewhere.

I called Joey Vallone at the Yonkers P.D. He wasn't in the office, so I gave Christine a message for him.

"Christine, I just tried to call Joey. When you get a chance, could you call and give him a message for me?"

"Ray, I don't think I want to be a go-between for you and my cousin. After the incident at the restaurant, the last place I want to be is between the two of you."

"Christine, what happened at the restaurant was cleared up. Mike and I are on a case, and Joey's working it with us, so would you please just give him a message for me?"

Reluctantly, she said, "Okay, Ray, what do you want me to tell him?"

I opened the leather case with my shield and a police ID.

"Tell him only civilians call this a badge. We call it a shield. He'll know what I mean. Mike and I will be at his office around two p.m."

"Sure, but what—"

"I'll see you later, okay?"

When Mike and I met Joey at his office, he was talking on the phone. He motioned us to come in and sit down.

"Hey guys, thanks for the call. I got your message, Ray. It's understood. Here's what I got. I just got off the phone with my confidential informant. It seems he knows somebody who knows something about the shooting of that kid. I'm supposed to meet him in an hour down by Van Cortlandt Riding Academy. You guys want to come along?"

"Absolutely. Then we can go back and re-canvass the area around the crime scene."

"Why, Ray?"

"Joey, when we did the first set of interviews, there was a lady who was walking her dog. I thought she knew more than she said, and I wanted a do-over with her. Do you remember saying that something stunk about this case, Mike?"

"Yeah, I remember, and it still does."

"Well, I think we should pay the lady and her dog a visit."

"Can I come along for this?" asked Joey.

"Sure. Let's go."

We got to the riding academy in about twenty minutes, parked the cars, and waited. The snitch showed up and was ready to spill, but he wanted us to make the breaking and entering charge go away in return. We agreed to help him, but he was warned that if this was a setup, there'd be no place he could hide. The tip we got from the snitch sounded okay. Allegedly, a deal was going down later that night at the Hunts Point market around ten p.m. It seemed that two guys involved in the Crotona Park shooting, one of them Latino, had some unfinished business—like two kilos worth. They were supposed to meet with bodyguards since their last meeting at Crotona Park ended with them shooting at each other. The dead boy wasn't even mentioned. We cut the snitch loose and told him to lose himself for a few days.

We re-canvassed the five-block radius of Crotona Park. The first time we talked to the locals, the answers were all the same—nobody saw anything. To a cop, that translated into somebody seeing something, but fear lasted a long time if you were elderly or sick and some young punk was terrorizing you. We put up flyers that offered a reward for information that led to the arrest of the person or persons responsible for the shooting, but we got nothing. We went back to see the woman who walked her dog. At first, she stayed with her story that she hadn't seen anything.

"Look, ma'am; we're trying to find a drug dealer who shot and killed a nine-year-old boy."

She replied, shaking, "But I didn't see anything."

"Ma'am, you were right there. Did you see anything, notice anything strange, something familiar, anything at all? This boy's parents deserve justice and closure. They need to know who was responsible for their son's death. Do you understand? Just think about it. Do you remember anything, even if you don't think it's important?"

"Well, there were two men arguing near the park entrance. It was just daylight, and I think one of them was Spanish. He was young and kind of short. The other man was a little older. He was a white man, and I think he was a police officer."

"Why do you say that?"

"Because I'm pretty sure I've seen him in the area in his uniform. The Spanish man kept talking about a sack or something that sounded like that. That's really all I remember."

My eyes lit up like a Christmas tree. I knew something wasn't right about those .38 casings. Drug dealers don't use .38s. They use bigger guns.

"What are you thinking, Ray?"

"Not sure yet, Mike."

"Joey, what about you?" Mike asked.

"I make the Latino for my boy Reyes—the one I told you about, who I've been watching for months—but the other sounds like a cop."

"I don't think it matters at this point, but if Reyes is in with a cop, I want both of them. One is scum, the other tainted the shield, and one of them killed the boy."

"I'm with you, Mike."

"I hear you both, and the Leung boy's parents need to know we got the guy who killed their son. Mike? Ray? Are we good for this?" We both nodded, and Mike said, "Oh yeah, and

I think it's time we talk to the lieutenant. We'll show him what we got and see if he'll approve a stakeout."

We cleared it with the lieutenant and coordinated the stakeout at Hunts Point. It involved the lieutenant, Mike, Joey, me, and uniformed backup just in case the perps decided to get brave.

We got to the market area at about seven p.m. and waited it out. It was all we could do. The market area was where the hookers hung out. Guys went there and got some semblance of privacy while they got their rocks off in the back seat of the car. It was quick and dirty—slam bam, thank you, ma'am. When you're on a stakeout, the minutes seem like hours. I thought about things like, "If I got hit, who would wear my shield? Was this just another battle in a war we couldn't win?"

It was quiet, almost deafening. The noise didn't bother me, but the silence did. This stakeout reminded me of guard duty in Vietnam. I almost wished something would happen because the quietude was killing me. My eyes played tricks on me. Faces appeared in the trees, but they didn't always move. The Viet Cong could have been five feet away, and you'd never know it. Here, the faces appeared in the shadows. Most times, it was nothing, but you couldn't think of it in those terms. You were in a combat zone. The difference was that this enemy wasn't fighting to keep its homeland.

They were trying to infect our schools and neighborhoods with drugs. They were not patriotic like the Viet Cong. They just wanted to put a bullet in you. The night was warm for March, but then it was a crazy month. You didn't know if it was going to be cold, hot, snowy, or rainy. Just then, we saw a car pull up. The driver got out and closed the car door with a thud. The car was big. Only Cadillacs and Lincolns had doors on them that made a thud. A few minutes later, a second car pulled up. The car was smaller. It looked like a Honda. It was just after ten p.m. The driver of the second car got out and left his door open. The two men talked, but it quickly escalated to shouting. My first instinct was to let them both kill each other; however, before either of them pulled a piece, the lieutenant got on the bullhorn:

"This is the police! Put your hands where I can see them, and get on the ground with your hands behind your back. Do it now!"

In the blink of an eye, the perps fired on us, and we returned fire immediately. The shootout ensued in an exchange of firepower that reminded me of skirmishes with the Viet Cong. It seemed like hours, but only two minutes had passed. One of the perps must've been wired to the hilt because he came out from behind a dumpster and drew two guns, fired continuously, and screamed at the top of his lungs. Joey moved from the driver's side of the unmarked to the front of the car, leveled his Glock, pumped two rounds into the perp's chest, and dropped him in his tracks. The shots continued for another thirty or forty seconds.

Mike moved toward the rear of the radio car as he tried for a clear line of fire. He leaned on the trunk for support, leveled the twelve gauge, and pumped out four shots. The second perp returned fire and hit Mike in the shoulder. I thought, "Oh my God. Don't let him be dead." I rushed over to him amid the continuous back-and-forth firing. I reached for my radio and called in a "10-13" for Emergency Services. The perp heard the officer down and took off running under a hail of gunfire by detectives and uniformed cops alike. When a fellow cop got hurt, it wasn't pretty, but he had his brothers to help him. I heard sirens coming from all over. They were there in a matter of minutes. I made sure the paramedics tended to Mike, and I went after the perp. He shot my partner.

I wanted him down for that. I tracked him to an abandoned building about three blocks away. I entered the building about as quiet as a sapper coming through barbed wire. He was there. I felt his eyes on me. I didn't have the lieutenant's bullhorn, so I made every word of my rapidly breathing chest count.

"Come out where I can see you. You have no way out of here. You won't be hurt. Just keep your hands where I can see them!"

The perp threw out his gun.

"Now, come out slowly, hands where I can see them!"

Imagine my surprise when he came out, and I found myself looking into the eyes of my former partner, Zack Tillman.

"Hello, Ray. Nice to see you," he said sneeringly. "Can I put my hands—"

"Don't move—not one inch, or I swear to God; I'll put the whole clip in you."

"Take it easy, Ray. We're friends."

"We were never friends. I just rode with you for six years. You shot my partner—"

"You won't shoot me, Ray. It's not in you. You're too much of a boy scout."

"Who shot the kid, Zack?"

"Reyes did. We had a deal, and he screwed up. I tried to hit him in the knees, but he fired back and hit the kid. Didn't mean for that to happen, Ray."

"Yeah, that'll make his parents feel real good. Enough talk. You know the drill. Hands behind your back."

I opened my cuffs and secured one of his hands. As I went to cuff his other hand, Zack went for my gun. As we struggled for control, all my thoughts were scattered. I thought about my rookie days, my tour of duty in Vietnam, and the survival skills that I learned: scan, don't stare. Never give up your service weapon. You can't afford to lose a fight or give up ground. The gun went off, and Zack jumped back. Neither of us was hit. I leveled my weapon at his head. An eighth of an inch was all that was between him and death. He started to laugh.

"You can't even shoot me, can you? You're such a freakin' boy scout, Ray."

In the blink of an eye, every ounce of rage I had in me was focused on the gun at his head.

My hand came down and smacked him on the side of his face, knocking him to the ground. I cuffed his other hand, brought him to his feet, and slammed him up against the wall to knock the fight out of him. I got in his face to give him a personal message.

"You not only killed an innocent boy, but you also shot my partner—a cop worthy of being a partner. You scarred the profession, and you disgraced the shield. You make me sick. Now move, or I swear to God I'll pump you full of holes."

I grabbed Zack by the collar and almost had to carry him. It would probably have been easier to kill him than carry him. As I half-stepped toward the door, Joey called out.

"Ray, you in there?"

"Over here, Joey," I replied.

"You got him. Way to go."

"How's Mike?"

"He'll be all right. He took one in the shoulder—he's asking for you."

Zack then tried to plead his case to Joey, but it landed on deaf ears.

"Please. You gotta help me. He beat me. You gotta protect—"

"Shut up, you piece of shit," Joey said.

"Joey, let me introduce you to my former partner, Zack Tillman."

"I'll be damned. Mike was right—a cop. Oh man, I'm going to enjoy kicking your ass!"

"Get in line, Joey. I got him first."

Zack cried like a schoolboy.

"You guys can't do this—I got rights!"

"Do what?" Joey said. "We were trying to help you off the stack of pallets, and you fell. Gee, that must've hurt. What do you think, Ray?"

"I think he just has to watch where he walks, especially now."

We got back to the stakeout area, and I turned Zack over to the uniformed cops.

"Joey, I have to—"

"I know, Ray, go ahead. I'll talk to you tomorrow. Say hey to Mike. Tell him some guys will do anything to get out of work and give my love to Christine."

"Why don't you stop by the station and tell her yourself?"

"Maybe I will. Good working with you."

"Same here, Joey, and thanks."

"No thanks needed, Ray. Only civilians call it a badge." And he smiled.

I went right over to the hospital. They had just brought Mike into his room from recovery. Katie was there with their oldest daughter, Jennifer. I walked in, and they both threw their arms around me in tears.

"It's all right," I said. "He's going to be fine."

We all kind of converged around Mike's bed.

"Did you get him?" Mike asked.

"Yup. One of the perps was a cop—my old partner, Zack Tillman."

"Did you kill him, Ray?"

"No, but I thought about it. He almost had me there for a minute."

"I knew there was something fishy about this case, Ray."

"Did you think it was a cop, Mike?"

"I thought so, but it could've been some kid with a Saturday night special just as easy."

"You're right about that."

"You got good instincts, Ray."

"Nah, I just had good training—from you."

"You'd have been fine. You were protected."

"By who, Mike, God?"

"Yes. God protected you. I knew that from the first moment we met."

"How'd you know that?"

"What's your shield number?"

"Come on, Mike, you know."

"Tell me, Ray."

"4-3-7-5-2-6-1. And?"

"All those numbers equal 7."

"So, what does that mean?"

"I believe it was ordained by God that you would be shielded from harm."

"So do I, Ray," Katie said.

"I don't know if I believe that, Mike."

"Think about it, Ray. You've struggled your whole life with so many things. You even hit rock bottom a few times, and through it all, you managed to survive. Do you really think it was all just a coincidence? You were poor and hungry as a child, but you didn't starve to death. You got wounded during the war, but you didn't die. You had a bad marriage, but you have a daughter who turned out to be a fine young woman. You've lived day by day, dollar to dollar, but you always managed to take care of things, and you even made a few friends along the way. And here tonight, you could've killed Zack Tillman, but you didn't. You're not a killer. You're a police officer, and you wear shield number 4-3-7-5-2-6-1. Call it what you want, but as bad as it's been, Ray, you've been shielded by God all your life."

"So, what do I do now, Mike?"

"Do what you've always done—take what you know, do the best you can, and leave the rest up to the Almighty because none of us is strong enough to do it alone."

"What will you do?"

"I think I'm going to call it a day. I've done the best job I can, and now it's your turn to help someone else along."

"You're ready, and you were ready when you chose to let the law judge Zack Tillman. It's your turn to drive, Ray."

"But where to, Mike?"

Chapter Twelve: Home Again—for the First Time

Just as Mike suggested, I continued on the job until I put in my twenty. I can't complain. I did well as a detective, using what Mike and the job taught me, but what do I do with these skills? I'm too young for a retirement community and too old to start a rock band, so what do I do with myself now that I'm retired? I thought the best choice for my next career was teaching, so I decided to become an adjunct professor.

Emily graduated from college with a teaching degree, and then she married a nice young man she met after teaching for a few years. They live in Pennsylvania just over the New Jersey border. I see them now and again, mainly over the holidays, but for the most part, they have their own lives now.

My father passed away while I was still on the job. It sounds terrible for me to say, but my mother will now have some peace in her life. I see her as often as I can, which I'm sure is not nearly enough. Mama gets lonely, even though she's friendly by nature and people like her.

My brother Joe died a few years ago at the hand of a drunk driver. Even though we were never really close, I somehow always knew that the streets would take him in the end. Joe spent his life running numbers, playing numbers, gambling at poker, and making shady deals. I wish we'd been close, but no two brothers could have been more different from the onset. The streets cut his young life too soon. My mother, now in her eighties, grieved over him for years. In all honesty, I don't think she ever stopped grieving over him.

Now and again, I've tried to look up old friends, but the more I looked for them, the more I found that I didn't have many old friends. I did manage to connect with my old bandmate, Tom, who surprisingly still played guitar. He was living down in Florida with more sunshine than anyone should handle, but he loved it.

So where did I end up? Well, I found myself an upscale place to live and ended up right back where I started—Yonkers. The only difference was I wasn't living under my father's rule anymore, and a sigh of relief came over me. Things were pretty much the same in Yonkers as I caught a few breaths of my hometown—the butcher, the baker, and the troublemakers. Still, there was something in the air that was unfamiliar. As I awake in Yonkers once again, I keep wondering why I am here in this place from which I ran away.

Christine and I are still dating, with the brass keeping a close eye on both of us. It's like they're waiting for us to do something wrong. Since I'm retired, it doesn't bother me that they have nothing better to do than to spy on us, but it does stress Christine. I guess working inside the precinct with all eyes on you would stress out anyone. Christine and I got into a deep discussion about how stressful her job was, with all the higher-ups watching to see if this thing we have interfered with either of our jobs. Truth be told, neither of us said anything to each other while we were on duty, but she was stressed enough that it manifested into depression.

"Are the brass still upsetting you, babe?" I asked.

"Yes, and one of them even said that I should end our relationship before any problems arise."

"Is that what you want to do?"

"God, no. I love you, and I don't want us to end."

"Do you want to get some counseling? I'd be happy to go with you."

"Maybe. I'm so tired of feeling so low all the time."

"Well then, let's go find a counselor. I hate seeing you so sad."

"I'm sorry, Ray. I'm so overwhelmed with the stress that comes from working at a police precinct, and it brings me down."

"No reason to apologize, Chris. It could happen to anyone. I certainly wouldn't like it if I worked in the precinct all day, every day."

After a long and arduous Internet search, we found a counselor who was not connected to the Police Department, and we began seeing her every week. We had our first visit shortly after making the appointment.

"Hello. I'm Anne Daly."

"I'm Ray MacDonald, and this is my sweetheart, Christine Fardella. I explained the issue briefly over the phone when I made the first appointment. Beyond that, I think Christine should elaborate on the issue at hand."

"Okay, Christine, what seems to be the problem?"

"I'm not sure that I'm comfortable talking to a perfect stranger about the problem I have."

"Ray, perhaps you should clear the air if Christine is comfortable with it."

Christine nodded.

"We both worked for the police department in the same precinct, and romantic relationships between co-workers are frowned upon. Since Christine works at the precinct all day, she is constantly being watched by the brass, even though I am retired from the force."

"Does that pretty much sum it up, Christine?"

"Yes, except that it causes me extreme stress. It has been suggested that I end the relationship with Ray, but I love him, and I don't want to do that."

"That's commendable, Christine. Have you spoken to your commanding officer and advised him or her that Ray is now retired?"

"Yes, Anne, but he already knew that since he was at Ray's retirement party."

"Have you spoken to anyone in Human Resources?"

"Not yet. I'm afraid to make waves."

"That would be my first suggestion. Let me know how that turns out. You're going on a cruise next week, so let's meet on the Monday after you return, Okay?"

It wasn't bad for a first session. At least it's a beginning. Christine seemed so fragile in front of the counselor. I thought she was going to have a breakdown right there in the office. I think maybe I'll buy her something really nice and unexpected and give it to her on the cruise.

I dropped in on Emily before our Caribbean cruise to see what she thinks about her father going into the field of higher education. I was excited about my vacation with Christine and couldn't wait to get her away from the office for a change. Next stop, the Bahamas, and nothing but fun!

Here we are on the cruise—beautiful ocean, beautiful ship, and so much to do that we can't do everything without running out of time. Christine and I are "taking it easy," so to speak. No shuffleboard and no hot, sweaty sports for us. We both like the sweet music and dancing over dinner. It's a bit laid-back, but we like it that way.

Ah, the Bahamas! We took the shuttle from the boat to the hotel. All the while, the bellhops and other hotel employees did their level best to make us feel welcome. Christine and I both signed in to separate but adjoining rooms. After dinner that night, we went for a walk and we talked a bit.

All of a sudden, she asked, "Ray, do you love me? You've never said it."

"Well, I know the cruise doesn't prove it, but maybe this will prove that I love you." Right there, I pulled a little box out of my pocket that contained a pear-shaped diamond ring with two baguettes. I thought Christine was going to faint when she saw it.

"Oh, Ray, is it real?"

"As real as real can be. Would you mind marrying me very much?"

"Oh yes, yes, Ray! I'll marry you, and I'll be a good wife."

"I have no doubt, Chris. I just want you to be you. Now let's see if the brass has any remarks when they see the ring."

"It's so beautiful, Ray."

"I'm glad you like it. You deserve it."

We went back to my room, where we must've kissed goodnight a hundred times, and then fell asleep in each other's arms. The rest of the cruise was great. Christine was not so stressed, and she actually allowed herself to have fun. I guess the ring did it.

Back in Yonkers, we had a hundred things to do—phone calls to make to announce our engagement, as well as picking the maid of honor, best man, and wedding party. I called Mike to ask him to be my best man. He was so happy for Christine and me, and he agreed to be my best man. There was still so much to do, like picking the ushers, securing the hall, hiring a DJ, and lots of other stuff. I think I need to do some praying before the whole wedding overwhelms me like a tidal wave.

Before Mike left the job, he tried hard to get me to depend on God more. I was used to just working things out for myself and never asking for anyone's help, but asking God for help makes sense. I didn't always feel that God was in my life. A combination of my mother, my aunt, and uncle, and Mike persuaded me to pray more to communicate with God. It sounded good, and I did feel better when I prayed.

When I look back at my life, high school brought memories of a new brand of cruelty. I had one date and three friends. They were in the rock band we started. The drummer was killed in a car crash. No one seemed to know what happened to the bassist, as he just drifted off somewhere. The other guitarist and I are still friends to this day. If it weren't for the band, I don't think I'd have survived high school. When I prayed, I started asking God, "Why this and why that?" I could no longer put up with being made fun of, so I left high school on my sixteenth birthday. My mother was disappointed because she so wanted me to finish my education. My father couldn't care less.

I was taught as a child that God is always with us, so where is God when He is nowhere to be found? It's not like I could've picked up a telephone and called Him. Sometimes I feel God is near when I think about my partner Mike or my mother, but most times, it feels like He is distant. I don't know what to think.

I got a call saying my mother passed away. The angels came while she was sleeping. I had so many things to talk to her about—things like now that Emily's a young lady, how do I deal with a female child who's grown up? While she was growing up, I spent as much time with her as humanly possible, but there were still so many things I didn't know. And now, I couldn't imagine getting married without my mother, but it brings me joy to know how happy she was for Christine and me after we told her the good news.

I made all the arrangements for my mother's funeral and notified everyone my mother knew, as well as the governmental agencies that administered her checks. As difficult as it was, I tended to all the necessary business while also helping Christine plan our wedding. It's only been a few days since my mother's passing, but God is good and merciful, so I kept praying.

After my mother's funeral and everyone went home, I broke down and wept for the loss of my mother. She always knew what to do. Mike taught me to ask God to come into my life and make changes, but I had to pray for these things to happen. Maybe God doesn't just do things. I have to pray and trust Him. I spent so many years doubting Him, but there is a God because I have felt His presence many times. Too many things have happened to make me believe otherwise. How did I survive the war without His grace in my life? And what about all the years I was protected as a policeman? Without God, I could never have survived such a turbulent childhood. I need Him in my life to be as close as a best friend.

Maybe if I talk to God in His house, He might answer me in a clearer way. I'm not a fool to think God would talk to me, but maybe there would be a sign. At least, that's what Mike used to say. Maybe I should've listened to Mike a lot more often.

I don't have a church per se, and the only one I was familiar with was the Catholic Church I attended as a boy. It's as good as any church, but I haven't been a practicing Catholic of late. I knew of St. Mary-by-the-Sea Church on Yonkers Avenue. After finding a rare parking space nearby, I walked up to the church and luckily found the doors open. I made my way to a pew near the altar. No sooner did I sit down, and a priest came over to me? He asked if I came to the church for a special reason.

"No, Father. I just needed to talk to God and hopefully get an answer."

The priest offered up his hand. "I'm Father Penna, Joe Penna. What's yours?"

"MacDonald. Ray MacDonald."

"Is there anything I can help with, Ray?"

"I don't know, Father. I've been racking my brain my entire life trying to figure out when God answers my prayers."

He smiled. "Ray, yours is not a problem. God always answers prayers. Sometimes He just says no, and He has His reasons."

"Father Joe, what possible reason would He have to say no?"

"Ray, sometimes God says no to keep us safe within His boundaries."

"Father, I was just trying to find out if God was distant from me."

"Ray, maybe you're distancing yourself from God. You seem angry at God. Have you ever examined why you're so angry at Him?"

"Father, you have no idea."

"Well then, clue me in, Ray."

"All right then, let's start out with something good—my mother. She died a few days ago. She taught me about God and all the rules the Catholic Church has."

"I'm sorry to hear about your mother, Ray. Continue with your story."

"Okay. Ever since I was little, the only thing I knew in our family was poverty,

humiliation, public assistance, and an abusive father who didn't like to work to support his family."

"That's a lot of anger to carry around, Ray."

"You bet it is, and I was looking to God to make things better. My mother was devoted to the church, so much so that we called her 'Sister Mary Catholic' because there was mass every day and a novena every night."

"So, why did you come to church today, Ray?"

"Because I'm tired of being angry, and all I want are answers."

"What are the answers you're looking for, Ray?"

"Why didn't God help my family? Why did we have it so hard? Why did He allow my father to beat us? Why did we go hungry? Why was I humiliated in school so much that I had to quit school just to make the jeering stop? Why didn't He hear our cries when we went hungry? Why, Father? Tell me."

"I don't know the answers, Ray. I can only say it's not fair to blame God when your father had much to do with your family's situation. Man is born with a sinful nature, and because God gave man free will, then it is up to man to make personal choices. You said it yourself, Ray, your father chose not to work. That was his choice and not one that God made."

"But what about the rest of it, Father—the poverty, the humiliation, public assistance, and my abusive father? What about all that?"

"Ray, you can't blame God for the mistreatment by others. As I said earlier, we are all born with a sinful nature. We all make personal choices, and that means everyone from your father to the kids at school who poked fun at you."

"Well, it doesn't explain everything, Father. How do you explain that I had no friends while I was in the military?"

"Ray, some people hate for no reason. Not everybody is going to like you, and vice-versa. Is what I'm saying starting to make sense to you?"

"Yeah, Father, some of it, but it doesn't explain everything."

"I'm sure it doesn't, Ray, but it's a good beginning. Maybe if you pray to Jesus and ask Him to remove the bitterness from your heart, He just might surprise you, and His answer may just put a smile on your face once you get rid of the king-size chip on your shoulder. Let's pray together, Ray, and remember that God loves you—always."

"Sure, Father. You lead."

I felt better after I prayed with Father Joe. He suggested that I do some positive things, like calling my daughter and going to lunch with a close friend. He also said that I should pray often and ask God to forgive my sins. I slept well that night, probably better than I've slept in years. As I awoke the next morning, the world didn't look any different to me, but I felt like a new me. Gone was the angry young man of so many years, and I somehow felt different. A peace came over me, and there seemed to be no room for anger or resentment. I can't explain it except to say that it must be God at work. I kept thinking over and over how easy it was to feel this way after all those years of being angry at God. I needed to find a church of my own where Christine and I would feel comfortable, so I poked around.

By chance, I ran into an old friend who went to the same church as my mother. He told me about a new church that he and the family were attending. He painted a very vivid, positive picture of it and suggested that I stop by one Sunday. I decided to go on Easter Sunday. When I walked through the door, I thought it was a rock concert. Oh my God, what kind of place is this? They had a stage complete with electric and acoustic guitars, a synthesizer, a piano, a set of drums, and three vocalists, along with words to the songs up on a big screen so that the whole church could sing along. I didn't know what to think, so I found a place to sit down and dig in.

Most of the sermon was centered around the resurrection of Christ from Matthew twenty-eight. Now, I don't know my Bible all that well, but I listened most intently. After the service was over, everyone moved from the sanctuary to a large room that could double as a soccer field. I felt a strange sense of welcome in a room full of people I didn't know. I smiled, and people came up to me, asked me my name, and asked general questions about what I thought of the service. I answered honestly but didn't offer up too much information.

Eventually, I found my old friend with his family in tow amid the crowd. We talked for a bit, and he asked me if I'd come back again for worship. A definite 'yes' formed on my lips, and I did mention that at first, I was a little taken aback by all the music, but I settled in pretty well. On the way home, I kept thinking about the whole experience in the church. I'd never been in a church like that, but I felt comfortable there. I may not know where to go next, but I have found a church of my own. Was it my friend or God who led me here? My brain was on fire with a plethora of thoughts and questions. I've spent years thinking and questioning why the Lord wasn't answering my prayers immediately. But He has more than me to watch over. Scripture teaches us that God is love. He is a guide and not a stormtrooper. That evening, as I read my Bible, I started to grasp hold of things that I never bothered to give much thought to before.

I have returned to that church every Sunday since, and the feeling is the same every time. I even took advantage of a few classes that were offered by the church. I also found a new friend at the church with whom I can talk guitars, and that is priceless. Slowly I can feel myself learning more and more about my Christian faith. I'm really excited to share everything I've learned with Christine.

As far as the subject of answering my prayers is concerned, I'm starting to develop a bit more patience. My prayers are always answered, but I have learned that sometimes God says 'no' or "not right now." When He says 'no,' I've heard it said that it's the Lord's way of keeping us within the realm of His protection. I guess "not right now" means that what I'm praying for isn't good for me right now. I don't understand it, but I accept it as the Lord's decision. To wait upon the Lord has to be the hardest thing we do as Christians.

Yonkers is different in some ways. My family has passed away, as well as the dock dogs, Byron and Abbey, and the people I knew are all gone from the Island. I miss all of them. My apartment in Yonkers is comfortable enough to call 'home' for Christine and me after we're married, but it won't be for the long term. Once we're settled after the wedding, we plan to buy a house. We haven't talked about having children yet, but we still have some time. As I look around, I see my life begin again, and it is all the Lord smiling down and blessing Christine and me with His infinite grace. I'm starting a new life with the woman I love, and everything looks positive.

There are so many things to think about now that Christine has said yes to being my wife. We've set the wedding date for a nice warm day in May. We already booked the hall, hired the caterer, and secured a great DJ who plays all the music we love.

Gone are the days of anger and frustration. I am at peace with the Lord. I gave my life over to Him, and He has blessed it with the fruits of love and peace. I don't worry if my prayers will be answered. I just wait upon the Lord and trust Him until He answers.

My disillusionment with the idea of home is gone, as Christine and I will decide where home is. Since I've gotten into the habit of doing it every day, perhaps I should just pray and ask the Lord for everything, or maybe I should just go wherever the Lord leads me since He has given me love and peace and has led me home again—for the first time.

~The End~

Made in United States
North Haven, CT
25 August 2023

40742012R00098